MW01241718

The Innocent for the Guilty

SANDI REBERT

DRAMATIC DIFFERENCE PUBLICATIONS

To Gladys,
You are a blessing to others just by your presence.
Your sweet, glowing love for Christ is an inspiration.

Acknowledgments

A huge "Thank you" to my husband, Brian, and my good friend, June White, for their encouragement and excellent editing skills. Also, many thanks to my wonderful launch team. You are the best! Most of all, I want to give glory to my Lord and Savior, Jesus Christ! He is the reason I write!

CHAPTER 1

A New Start

1891

The strain of three riders and the supplies loaded quickly in the dark of night was almost too much for the small, rickety wagon. Troy had been concerned that the noisy squeaking of the cart's wheels as it clattered and shivered down the dusty road would draw attention when they first left Tuscon. Instead, it surprised and relieved him that no one had followed, or so it seemed. The brush tied to the back of the wagon had successfully covered their tracks, and he and his family were now safely away from Rod's revenge.

Several years earlier, Troy had heard about Spring River from a peddler. It had been described as a "very out-of-the-way location in the middle of nowhere." What better place for a new start? Wyoming was two states away from the territory of Arizona. Sheriff Wilson wouldn't send anyone after them; in fact, the sheriff was the one who had told them to leave town, even helping to pack the wagon. Still, Troy worried that a report would be sent by telegraph associating him with the recent horrific event. Would the sheriff in Spring River have the authority to arrest him?

The journey had been a strange encounter with time. Though advancing one hour into the future due to the time zones used by the railroads for the past eight years, the family of three went back in time seasonally. Spring was just around the corner when they left Arizona at the beginning of February. As they proceeded farther north, winter weather caught the weary travelers in its snowy web more than once. Now that they had arrived at their destination, more than a month later, the first budding of trees was still a few weeks away.

It was a cow town, much smaller than Tucson, with a livery, saloon, and a hotel—at least the sign above the weather-worn front door stated it was a hotel. Even though it boasted two stories, Troy guessed the small wooden structure would have only a handful of rooms available. Nevertheless, it reminded him that he and his family needed a place to stay and, as his growling stomach affirmed, food to eat. The difficulty was that they had no money. He would need to find a job first. Scratching his head, Troy wondered if such a thing would be possible to find in such a two-bit town.

Farther down the main street, which, from his observation, was the only street, they passed a small post office that, according to the sign, was also the telegraph office. Next to it was a doctor's office and a tailor shop. Troy noticed that only a few houses lined the street. He guessed most people lived on outlying ranches like the two they had passed on their way into town. A small church that he presumed doubled as a schoolhouse was at the far end.

Troy pulled on the reins, stopping the horse in front of the general store with a sign above the door that read Mom and Pop's Mercantile. A customer exited with a bundle under one arm and a baby in the other.

"There's a notice in the window, Mama. Says, 'Help Wanted.' I'll go in and see if I can get me a job."

"Are you sure we're far enough away?" Mary's voice was quivery, as it always got when she was nervous.

"I think so. We need the money. Even if I can work for just a few days or so, it'll help us fill our stomachs. We can't go on without eating." He flashed one of his big grins that always melted her heart. "Pray for me, Mama."

"I will, son. God has promised to meet our needs."

Troy clambered out of the wagon, tipped his hat to an elderly woman passing by, then tied the horse to the hitching post. Glancing around to be certain they hadn't been followed, the sound of creaky hinges caught his attention. Looking to his left, he couldn't help but see the sign waving in the rustling breeze from the building three doors down. The letters stood out to him as if they were a mile wide—Sheriff's Office.

A sudden tenseness arose in his throat. The gnawing pain in his stomach was magnified by the delicious smell of freshly baked bread wafting across the street from a homey-looking café. He brushed off his clothes even though, being covered in trail dust, it would do little to improve their condition. He knew he reeked of sweat from days of travel, but, despite his physical appearance, smell, and lack of confidence, he straightened his shoulders and opened the door.

At the counter, an attractive young lady was paying for some linen. Troy glanced down at his shabby britches and patched coat. He felt coarse and insignificant compared to her.

The shopkeeper cast a furtive glance in his direction; Troy lowered his eyes and pretended to examine a barrel of apples. The owner led his customer to the back of the store, showing her some items she'd inquired about.

Since it seemed as though the girl's purchase would take a while, Troy took the opportunity to explore his surroundings. It was a typical mercantile with shelf after shelf of canned goods, calico, broadcloth, sewing notions, crocks, dishes, and tools. A small table of soaps and spices gave the air an aromatic fragrance despite the thick layer of dust that had settled over almost everything. A rounded showcase displayed medicines, pistols, and rifle shells. Buggy whips, harnesses, tools, and farming implements hung on the walls. Rifles were kept in a locked cabinet with a glass door. Copper pots, iron kettles, and pails dangled from the ceiling, seemingly competing for space with various sizes and shapes of lanterns. There were bins of vegetables and fruits. Stacked in the front left corner near the window were sacks of flour, sugar, and grain. Sitting on the counter beside the cash register were three big glass jars filled with penny candy, a coffee mill, scales, and brown wrapping paper. Next to the apple barrel was one containing pickles, another with crackers, and one filled to the brim with potatoes. A pot-bellied stove in the center of the store revealed what he had always heard about this area of the country—even though the summers could be exceedingly warm, spring and fall could be frosty, and winters bitterly cold. Near the stove were a rustic table and two caned chairs already set up for the next game of checkers. A staircase in the back left corner led to an upstairs door. As Troy turned around and walked to the front of the store, he noticed another door directly to the right of the counter and assumed it led to the small room that extended to one side of the store's front porch.

The gnawing returned, twisting like a knife inside him and melding into a queasy sensation that felt like it would rise in his throat and choke him. He tried not to think about it, impatiently hoping the young lady would leave. At last, he heard her quiet steps, the rustle of her cotton skirt across the rough wooden floor, and the creaking and banging of the door as it opened, then shut.

Immediately, the old shopkeeper was at his side. "Somethin' I can be helpin' ya with, boy?" His voice conveyed suspicion.

Troy wondered if a picture of himself *had* circulated and the shop owner knew who he was. "I—I saw the sign in your window, sir."

"Oh?" The man's eyes squinted from behind small wire-rimmed glasses perched precariously on the tip of his long crooked nose.

Troy felt as though the deep brown eyes were piercing through his own. It made him feel agitated and nervous. "Yes, sir. Says you need help."

The man rubbed his thick gray beard. "And ya figure yer the one to give it, do ya?"

4

"I—I need it, sir."

"Well ..." the old man snorted, scrutinizing Troy from head to foot. He caught Troy's gaze again with a discerning stare. "From the looks of ya, I'd say ya do." He stroked his beard again. "I—ah don't recall seein' ya around these here parts before."

"You ain't, sir. Me and my family just got into town today."

"I see." He patted his beard this time as if it helped him think. "Ya look mighty young to be havin' a family," the man continued, still eyeing Troy distrustfully.

"I'm almost nineteen, sir, but I ain't married. I got my Mama and my sister with me."

"No pa?"

Troy shifted his eyes nervously to the floor. "No—no, sir."

"How do I know I can trust ya, boy?"

Troy's heart started racing. "I—I guess you don't, sir. But, if you just give me a chance, I'll prove it to you. I'm a hard worker, sir. I take orders real good and—and I don't complain none either."

"Hmph! Seems to me a boy of yer talents—if he was tellin' the *truth* ..." The old man arched one bushy eyebrow as he emphasized the word. "wouldn't be so hard up for a job."

Troy said nothing as the color rose to his cheeks.

"That yer family out there in yonder wagon?"

"Yes, sir."

"Well. I reckon ya'd best not keep them waitin' no longer."

Troy's shoulders sagged under the disappointing blow as the nagging pain in his stomach returned. Slowly, without looking at the shop owner, he shuffled toward the door.

"Hmph! Seems to me a boy what's jest got hisself a job would be a might happier!"

"What—what did you say?"

"Ya heard me. Now, if yer aimin' to please, go fetch that family of yers and bring 'em inside. I got a room fer my help. T'ain't much, but I reckon it's a heap better than that ol' wagon. Well, stop yer gawkin', boy, and get on with it afore I change my mind!"

"Y—yes, sir. Yes, sir!"

Troy ran out the door to the wagon. "Mama!" he exclaimed breathlessly. "I got it! I got the job!"

"Praise the Lord!" Mary exclaimed excitedly, clasping her hands together in delight and thankfulness. Troy reached up, put his hands around his mother's thin waist, and lifted her from the wagon.

The pile of blankets in the back jostled about until seven-year-old Angie poked her head out and peered at them through wide eyes. "Does that mean we get to eat?"

"We'll have a roof over our heads. There's probably a pump around here for water," Troy informed them.

"I'm starving, Troy! Please," Angie piped up.

"I'll—I'll see what I can do, Angie. Can't promise nothing."

"A room! Oh, Troy, I prayed for a room." A tear trickled down his mother's cheek.

"Did you pray for food, Mama?" Angie asked.

"Yes, dear, I did," Mary assured her.

"Then where is it?" Angie complained.

"Just be patient, Angie." Troy winked at his sister as he pulled the two worn carpet bags from the wagon. "Mama's prayers are always answered."

"Not always, Troy," Mary whispered to her son.

The disturbed expression on his mother's face brought to his mind painful recollections from long ago and fresh, haunting memories that tore at his soul. It wouldn't be good to linger on either of them. He glanced about the street; no sign of Rod or the town's sheriff. They were safe—for now.

The storekeeper ushered them through the door next to the counter into a small but cozy room. Mary was glad to see a window; a musty smell permeated the space, revealing it had been closed up for a while. She made a mental note to let in some fresh air as soon as the shopkeeper left them to themselves. The furnishings were simple but sufficient: a bed covered with a colorful quilt, a chest of drawers with a washbowl and pitcher, an oil lamp, a braided rug, a caned chair that matched the two in the shop, and a wood stove.

"Only got one bed," the old man muttered apologetically as he blew the dust off the old pine dresser. "Only expected to house one person, not a whole passel."

"It's wonderful, mister ..."

"Name's Williams, ma'am. Jeremy Williams, but folks 'round here jest call me 'Pop.' Reckon ya can do the same."

"It's wonderful, Mr. Williams. I mean, Pop. We're deeply grateful for the chance you're giving Troy."

"So that's yer name." Pop adjusted his glasses and peered up at the handsome young man, whose six-foot height cleared his own by five inches. "Ya never did tell me."

"I'm sorry, sir. Yes, my name's Troy. This here's my mother, Mary, and my sister, Angie."

"The girl looks a little peaked."

"She'll be fine, sir," Troy assured him.

"No, I won't, Troy. I'm hungry!"

Troy gave her a sideways glance. "Angie," he murmured under his breath.

"I can't help it, Troy!"

"I'm sorry, sir, I—"

"Sorry? Well, no need to be. Mom—she's my missus, she and I ain't had supper yet. I reckon she can add a little more water to the soup."

"Sir, I—"

"Now, son, ya said ya took orders real well."

"Yes, sir."

"Then don't argue with me, boy. Supper will be ready in about twenty minutes. Mom and I live above the shop. Jest mosey on up the stairs in the back corner."

"Yes, sir." Troy extended his hand. "I'm real grateful, sir."

The old man clasped the strong, rough hand in his feeble one. "I got a feelin' I'm the one who should be grateful. I like yer family. Yer a brave fellow to be lookin' after yer ma and sister, what with no pa." Realizing his emotions were showing, a thing Jeremy always tried to conceal under a crusty façade, he quickly jerked his hand away and into his pocket. "Mind ya now, boy, I ain't seen yet whether I can trust ya. Ya have to prove yerself."

Troy blushed again. "I understand, sir. I promise you won't be disappointed."

"Hmph! We'll see," Jeremy muttered as he hobbled away. "Ya might want to wash up a mite afore ya come to dinner," he called out to them as he started up the stairs. "Use one of them galvanized buckets from the shop. The well's in the middle of town. Soap and towels are in the dresser."

"Thank you, sir!" Troy called back, grinning. He knew all three of them were a sorry sight to behold.

"Maybe I'll have time to slip into a different dress," Mary said self-consciously.

Troy closed the door and glanced around the cramped quarters. He sighed. It was better than nothing. He couldn't help blaming himself that they'd had to leave home so quickly; he was sure they'd never be able to return.

"Troy," Mary slipped her hand into his. "Don't you think we should take a moment to thank the Lord for His provision?"

"Sure, Mama, sure," he responded.

CHAPTER 2

A Close Call

Dinner with Jeremy and Tess Williams was pleasant.

Tess was a sweet, amiable woman with soft green eyes and wispy gray hair pinned into a loose bun. Her winsome smile put everyone at ease immediately. From the way she doted on Angie, she obviously loved children.

Troy admired the elderly couple, whom he guessed were in their seventies. He'd never known his grandparents but decided he would have liked them to be similar.

Tess tucked a stray hair behind her ear. "Did ya have far to travel today?"

"We came quite a distance," Mary said, not wanting to give away too much information. "It felt good to get off the wagon. We're so thankful for the room."

"It ain't much. I wish we had more beds fer ya," Tess said regretfully.

"It's fine, ma'am," Troy piped up. "I can sleep on the floor. Mama and Angie can take turns sleeping on the chair and the bed."

"Are you all right, Angie?" Mary asked, noticing that her daughter, who had been so hungry, was hardly touching any food.

"I—I don't feel so good, Mama."

9

Mary reached over and felt Angie's forehead. "I believe she has a fever, Troy."

"I'd be glad to fetch the doc fer ya," Jeremy volunteered.

"No!" Mary and Troy answered quickly in unison.

"Thank you, sir. I'm sure she'll be fine," Troy stated optimistically.

"I'll take her down to the room so she can rest, Mama. You stay here and finish. You can bring our plates down later if that's all right with you, Mrs. Williams. We can return the dishes in the morning, or I can bring them up later tonight if you'd like."

"Mornin' will be jest fine, Troy. And, please, call me 'Mom.'"

She turned to Mary. "I have some sassafras tea that might be of help."

"That's very kind of you."

Troy gently helped Angie to her feet and held on to her as they descended the stairs. When they reached the last step, Angie collapsed. Troy quickly scooped her up in his arms, carried her to the room, and laid her on the bed. He felt her forehead; she was burning up. A doctor might be necessary, but they had no money. If Angie became delirious, as she often did when feverish, there was no telling what she might say. He needed wisdom and prayed for his mother to come soon.

It was only ten minutes until Mary arrived. "I couldn't wait to check on Angie. Mom said she'd bring the food to us. She made up some tea, and I wanted to get it into Angie as soon as possible. I hope it doesn't make her feel more nauseous. She didn't eat much. Her stomach has to be almost empty."

Angie started moaning; she was delirious. "Mama! Mama, where are you?"

"I'm right here, darling." Mary dipped a cloth in the wash bucket's cool water and placed it on Angie's forehead, then took her daughter's limp hand in her own.

"Mama! Don't let them hurt, Troy, Mama! Don't let them hurt him!"

Mary and Troy exchanged anxious looks.

"Shh, Angie. It's all right. No one's going to hurt your brother."

"They're coming, Mama! They're coming!"

"We've got to keep her quiet," Troy whispered nervously.

Angie began convulsing.

"What are we going to do?" Mary's look of fear pierced through his heart.

"I'm going to ask Pop about getting the doctor."

"No, Troy. It's too risky. We have no money. Besides, if she talks while he's here—"

"It has to be done, Mama. I'm not going to endanger her life to save mine."

"Oh, Troy." Mary stood up, buried her head on her son's chest, and wept.

Troy put his arms around her trembling form. "We need to be strong, Mama. It's just another time we need to put our faith to the test."

"God has tested our faith so much, Troy. I don't know if I can go on."

"Mama ..." He gently pulled her away from him and took hold of both her hands, looking her directly in the eyes, his own filled with compassion and admiration. "God has promised to work 'all things together for good.' Isn't that what you always tell me? I can't see good coming from any of this, but—"

"God sees the bigger picture," Mary finished. She knelt by the bed and began bathing Angie's forehead again.

"Poor little girl," Troy said compassionately. Suddenly, another child's face flashed through Troy's mind—that of a five-year-old girl lying motionless in a dark room. The troubling thought made him feel dizzy. He clenched his fists and tried to clear the disturbing picture from his mind.

"Mama, tell them Troy didn't do it! Tell them, Mama!"

"Shh. Don't worry, darling," Mary said, reassuringly patting her daughter's hand, "I will."

A knock on the door startled them. It was Mr. Williams. Not wanting him to hear anything Angie might blurt out, Troy opened the door barely wide enough to squeeze through.

"I was checking that the shop door was bolted and heard some sort of commotion goin' on," Jeremy said. "Everythin' all right?"

"My, ah—my little sister's fever is worse, sir."

"Ya goin' to fetch the doc?"

"I was thinking on it, sir."

"Well, don't jest think on it, boy! Git a move on!"

Troy put his hand on Jeremy's arm. "We can't pay him, sir."

"Never mind that. She's needin' a doctor. I'm sure I'll be able to spare ya to do some chores fer him after a while. I know the doc pretty well. He'll be considerin' that plenty enough pay." He rubbed his beard thoughtfully. "Tell ya what. I'll go fetch the doctor myself. It still gits chilly around here at night. Jest let me grab my duster, and I'm off."

"Would you like me to come with you, sir?"

"Ya think I can't walk fast enough or can't see well at night, boy? I know this town like the back of my hand. I'll get there quicker without ya." Then, his voice sympathetic, he added, "Ya stay with yer Ma and sister, Troy. They need ya."

"Yes, sir, and thank you."

"Anythin' I should tell doc besides the fever?"

"She's been delirious, had convulsions."

As if on cue, Angie started tossing and turning. Low moans escaped her parched lips. Troy thought quickly. He closed the door completely before his sister started talking again, in case she said something incriminating.

"If ya need more help," Jeremy added before heading outside, "ya fetch Mom. She's done lots of doctorin' in her time."

"Thank you," Troy responded, grateful for the offer yet knowing he couldn't take it.

Troy locked the shop door behind the old man, then returned to his mother's side. "We'd better start praying Angie keeps quiet while that doctor's here," he said as he dipped the cloth back in the water, then handed it to his mother.

Gently reapplying the cloth, Mary glanced up at Troy with a worried look and a catch in her throat. "It doesn't seem to be helping."

Troy paced back and forth across the small room a few times. He didn't know what to do. It would be better for Angie's sake if the doctor came quickly. Yet, if the doctor came too soon while his sister was still feverishly rambling, it could be disastrous for him—even fatal. He closed his eyes and took a deep, calming breath. His focus needed to be on Angie's health, not his welfare. Still, if something happened to either one of them, he worried that their mother wouldn't be able to bear the burden; she'd been through so much already.

His thoughts transported him back to the beautiful ten-room house he'd known as a young boy. It was a memory he wanted to keep yet needed to forget. Ever since they had to leave that house, he would try to picture it in his mind from time to time, to envision what life had been like before people discovered where his father had gotten his money. The two-story dwelling was embellished with massive pillars across the front and ornate marble fireplaces in every room. A curved staircase graced the grand entrance. The dining room table, with intricately carved legs and matching seats, was outdone only by the sparkling silver tea set and delicately patterned china. The parlor boasted a mahogany settee with velvet cushions. The bedrooms each had a four-poster bed, floral wallpaper, and gilded mirrors. The servants—a cook, butler, and housekeeper—added to the prestige that accompanied such finery. After his father went into hiding, their house was taken to pay back the money to the bank Colby had robbed.

They moved into a two-room shack five miles from town—just his mother and him, although his father came home occasionally. It had been eight years since he'd spent a few days at home. Nine months later, Angie was born. Then, shortly before they

13

were forced to leave Tucson, Colby came home for just a few minutes—long enough to ruin Troy's life.

Troy shook himself out of his reverie and looked at the small window, refocusing his mind on simple, everyday things that didn't matter but would take his attention off the dire situation engulfing them. *Mama could fix up some pretty curtains,* he mused. *And we could get this place cleaned up a little more.*

A loud knock on the shop door startled him from his contemplation. Instantly, his heart started pounding against his chest. The tormenting fear he'd faced intermittently during the last couple of months returned with a fury, gripping his mind and body in its clutches.

"It's all right," Mary assured him, "Angie's asleep."

Relieved, Troy sighed, then quickly walked into the shop just as Jeremy started knocking again. "It's me, boy. I brung the doctor."

"Just a minute, sir," Troy said as he fumbled with the key.

"It took yer long enough," Jeremy muttered when Troy finally opened the door.

"Sorry, sir."

"This here's Doc Caldor."

Troy nodded. "Thank you for coming, sir. I'm afraid we don't have any—"

"Stop," Jeremy whispered. "I told ya we'd work somethin' out."

"Yes, sir," Troy responded sheepishly.

"Right this way, Doc," Jeremy said as he led the doctor into the little spare room.

Doc Caldor examined Angie for a few minutes. "She seems to be all right now."

"Yes. Her fever broke not more than a few minutes ago. She was hallucinating before that," Mary answered.

"Mmm. You're fortunate it broke so soon. Or rather, I should say, she's fortunate. The longer a high fever continues, the greater the risk involved."

"I'm sorry you had to come all this way for nothing, doctor," Mary apologized.

"Nonsense. I don't live far away. Besides," he added good-naturedly, "Pop is overdue for a checkup, and I can never get him to come see me, so I reckon I had to come over here to see him!"

"Don't ya go to tinkerin' none with me! I'm doin' all right, and ya know it," Jeremy remarked. "Why, I could run circles around ya."

The doctor laughed good-naturedly. "You know something, Pop? I believe you could!"

He turned his attention back to Mary. "Since your daughter is sleeping peacefully, and Pop won't let me take a look at him, I guess I'll head on home. Be sure to send your boy to fetch me if she gets worse, ma'am, even if it's in the middle of the night."

"I will, doctor, and thank you."

"See that she gets plenty of rest and water. It would be best if she had lots of liquids for the next couple of days—not much solid food."

"Yes, thank you, doctor," Mary replied softly.

Troy followed the doctor and Jeremy as they left the room. "Sir, we don't have the money to pay you now, but—"

"Now, I told ya doc wouldn't mind if ya jest done a few chores fer him. Ain't that right, Doc?"

The doctor put his hand on Troy's shoulder. "Let's look at my first visit with your family as a 'welcome to Spring River' gift."

"You would do that?" Troy said in astonishment.

"Yes. Does that surprise you?"

Troy hung his head. "I'm—I'm just not used to people treating us with kindness, is all."

The doctor patted Troy's shoulder. "Well, I'm sorry to hear that. I hope you'll find the people of Spring River to be friendly."

"Thank you, sir," Troy replied, secretly wondering how long the welcoming spirit of the townspeople would last.

CHAPTER 3

Toby

T roy woke early the following day, eager to begin his new job and determined to make a good impression on his employer. However, knowing his first responsibility was to his mother and Angie, he took the bucket down to the town well first. The air was moist; a crisp breeze rustled his dark brown hair. It gave him a transitory and deceptive sense of freedom. Yet, the fear of being discovered still lingered threateningly over his head. Troy knew that Rod, in particular, would only give up the search for him once he was convinced it was futile. He glanced cautiously around at the buildings, some with false fronts, the store's name painted in large letters across the façade, others with sloped roofs and dormer windows, then down the road to each town entrance. To his relief, only a few people were stirring, and there was no sign of his pursuers.

Quietly leaving the bucket in their little room, Troy slipped into the shop, found a broom, and began sweeping the floor.

"Well now, that's what I like to be seein'—a man with ambition!" Jeremy cheerfully announced as he meandered down the stairs.

Troy smiled. "Good morning, sir."

"Good mornin'! That sister of yers feelin' better this mornin', is she?"

"Yes, sir. Praise the Lord."

Troy's mention of God caused the old man some consternation. He knew he'd soon need to talk with his new employee about religion. "Good. Good. Guess we wouldn't have needed ol' doc last night, after all, what with her fever breakin' afore he even got here."

Troy thought back to the previous night, remembering how close they had come to Angie inadvertently revealing their secret. "We prayed it would."

"About that," Jeremy said hesitantly. "I noticed ya prayed afore ya ate last night, too. Yer pretty religious, ain't ya—yer kinfolk, too."

"Well, sir, I don't know if I'd exactly call it religious. We know the Lord if that's what you mean."

"Yeah, that's what I'm meanin'. And that's a good thing, boy. Don't git me wrong. It's a good thing fer some folks, but me and Mom are happy jest the way we is." He knit his thick eyebrows together, "If'n ya knows what I mean?"

"Sir?"

"In other words, yer to keep yer religion to yerself. I don't want ya pushin' yer beliefs on us—or my customers, fer that matter. It ain't good fer business. Ya understand what I'm sayin', boy?"

Troy took the warning as a threat that he could lose his job, something he couldn't afford. Not now. He knew he must heed the man's orders; he must tread softly and be extra careful to please his employer, or he and his family could be out on the street without food, money, or home. "Yes, sir, I think I do," he said softly.

"Good. We'll git along jest fine! By the way, take a quick break and tell that mother and sister of yers to go upstairs and git some breakfast. Git some yerself while yer at it. I don't want my help keelin' over on the floor from hunger."

"Yes, sir! Thank you!"

Mary decided it would be best for Angie to stay in bed, so Troy brought down a platter of food.

"Look at this, Troy! Ham, potatoes, eggs, biscuits. We haven't eaten this well in I don't know how long."

Troy smiled. "Yes, ma'am," he replied, then lowered his eyes to the floor. It was true; they hadn't eaten that well since he was five.

The smell of food woke Angie out of her deep sleep. "I'm hungry, Mama."

"The doctor said you should have mostly liquids, honey."

"Please, Mama! I'm hungry!"

"Well, I guess it won't hurt you to eat a little. But, after such a bad fever last night, you need to take it slow."

"I will, Mama." Angie sat up in bed, greedily took the plate from her mother's hands, and stuffed an entire biscuit in her mouth.

"Not so fast!" Mary scolded.

"I'm hungry!"

"I know, darling, but you don't want to make yourself sick again."

Troy looked up and exchanged an anxious glance with his mother. That was an understatement. They couldn't risk Angie having another fever, for Troy's sake, as well as hers.

Troy hurried through his breakfast and returned to the store just as the first customer entered.

"Mornin', Emma," Pop said jovially.

"Good morning, Pop," the matronly Mrs. Tucker replied. "It's a beautiful day today! The sun is shining. You really ought to pull up that shade, Pop, and let some light into this store. It's hard to see what you've got!"

"You're right," Tess added, coming down the stairs to take her place behind the cash register so Jeremy could show Troy some items in the back that needed to be displayed in the store. "I'm always gittin' on him about that, too. He always forgits!"

Walking over to the display window, she raised one of the shades, then lowered it quickly. "Oh, no," she informed her husband. "Here comes Toby. It, sure enough, didn't take him long!"

She whispered a warning to Troy. "Toby Jenson's comin'!"

Puzzled, Troy wondered if the name was supposed to mean something to him. "Toby Jenson, ma'am?"

19

"The town's busybody," she informed him. "No doubt he heard about you already. He's gonna have a heap of questions fer ya." Wanting to protect Troy from Toby's prying ways, she winked at Jeremy, hoping he would immediately take Troy to the back room and get him out of sight. She liked the young stranger and knew, all too well, how relentless Toby could be when his curiosity was aroused.

It was too late. Toby was already in the store. "Mornin', Pop. Mornin', Mom. I had a few minutes to spare and thought I'd come visit with you for a spell."

Tess was already annoyed with him. "Any special reason, Toby?"

Toby strained his neck, trying to locate the newcomer he'd heard about. "Nothin' in particular. Just wonderin' ..."

Jeremy knew it was useless trying to hide Troy. Best for the boy to get the interrogation over with. He wondered how Toby had heard about the strangers. *Doc's wife,* he thought to himself. *She'd be the one! A regular meddler, that lady. Jest like Toby.* "He'd be over yonder by the pickle barrel, Toby."

Toby tipped his hat and shuffled over toward his prey.

"And jest in case ya'd like to know," Tess added, hoping to discourage Toby from his fact-finding mission, "he's got work to do."

"Yes, ma'am," Toby replied nonchalantly, "I'm sure he does."

Emma Tucker shook her head in disgust.

Once he spotted Troy, Toby didn't waste any time. "Hello, young fellow!"

Troy looked at him nervously and continued sweeping. "Sir."

"The name's Toby—Toby Jenson." Troy shook the plump hand extended to him by the tailor. An awkward moment of silence followed. "And your name would be?"

"Oh, sorry, sir. It's Troy."

Toby wasn't about to be satisfied with just a first name. "Troy what?"

Troy froze. Revealing his last name could possibly cost him his life.

"You *do* have a last name, don't you, boy?"

20

"Yes, sir. Of course, it's, ah ..." Troy was tempted to give a fake name but couldn't bring himself to lie. "Daniels, sir. Troy Daniels."

"Daniels, Daniels. Name sounds familiar, but I don't recollect no Daniels in these parts. Where did you come from?"

Troy knew he needed to be vague, especially since Toby recognized his last name. *Hopefully, he hasn't heard of Pa*, Troy mused, trying to encourage himself. "Arizona territory, sir."

Toby fingered his chin thoughtfully. "Arizona. Arizona. Long trip." He cleared his throat. "I hear it's just you, your ma, and your sister."

"Yes, sir." Troy noticed Jeremy motioning for him to help with the merchandise he was shelving. "If you'll excuse me, I think Pop has something for me to do."

Toby reached out, quickly grabbing Troy's arm before he could walk away. "Pop's a patient man. He'll wait. You got no pa, boy?"

Troy swallowed hard. The conversation was getting too risky. "Ah, no sir, not—not with us."

"Dead, is he?"

Troy's hands felt sweaty. "No, sir."

"Left your ma, did he? Too bad. Too bad. That happens from time to time. What did you say his name was?"

"Troy! I need ya to git somethin' off the top shelf." Mom's call for help rescued Troy from revealing any more.

"Coming, ma'am. Excuse me, Mr. Jenson." He shook his arm loose from Toby's grip and strode swiftly to the front of the store. "Thank you," he whispered to Tess.

Mom chuckled. "Anytime, Troy. And I have a feelin' there will be lots more!"

Troy's six-foot frame allowed him to retrieve the item easily. He handed it to Tess, but not before Toby was at his side again.

"How old are you, boy?"

Emma had heard enough. She was also curious about the new arrival but detested nosy people. She finished paying for her groceries, then turned to the tailor in a fury. "Really, Toby, give the boy some room to breathe!"

21

"What are you talkin' about?" Toby answered in sheer ignorance.

Emma was incredulous. *How can people be so blind to their imperfections?* she wondered. "What am I talking about?" she sputtered. "You are the worst—I repeat, the worst busybody this town has ever seen! I suggest you get back to your work. There are enough people in this town to keep your tailoring business busy from sunup to sundown!"

"All right! All right! I'll leave!" Then, just before he closed the shop door, he stuck his head back inside and said directly to Troy, a sly smile on his ruddy, round face. "But I'll be back!"

CHAPTER 4

New Clothes

The rest of the morning passed quickly, with only a few patrons entering the store. However, by late afternoon, word had traveled about Pop's newly hired help. The little shop was bustling with people; some came to buy merchandise, some to pass the time playing checkers, and others just to "jaw," as Jeremy put it. Toby didn't return, but Troy still felt conspicuous since he was the center of attention. He was the stranger who'd come out of nowhere. Naturally, they were all interested in seeing what little tidbit they could discover about the young man and his family to add to the gossip doc's wife and Toby had already begun. Troy cringed under all the observation and kept his mouth closed as much as possible. When it was necessary to speak, he tried to answer the inquisitive townspeople carefully so as not to jeopardize himself.

Jeremy noticed Troy occasionally looking down at his ragged clothes, the rising color in his cheeks reflecting the humiliation he felt inwardly. Deciding to help his new worker feel less self-conscious, Jeremy closed the shop an hour early. "Well, boy," he remarked, slapping Troy playfully on the back. "Ya made it through yer first day in Spring River. Everythin' should be downhill from now on. Don't feel too bad 'bout bein' a spectacle today. Folks is hard up fer entertainment 'round here, and anythin' or anybody new livens things up a mite. Now that they's got their curiosity satisfied, I reckon ya'll soon blend into the wall like the rest of us. Come on. We're headin' to the tailor shop to git ya some new duds. Them rags yer wearin' ain't fit to be seen in public."

Troy blushed again and followed his employer to the tailor's, dreading another meeting with the pudgy, bald-headed snoop.

Toby's beady eyes glistened with anticipation as they entered the smoky shop. "Well, well, well. And what can I do for you *fine* gentlemen?" he asked with noticeable sarcasm.

Troy squirmed inwardly. He hoped the measuring wouldn't take long.

"The boy here needs some new clothes."

"I thought so. I thought so." Toby whipped out a measuring tape and began sizing up Troy. "How long have you been in these things?" he asked, hoping for more information to add to the collection of snippets about the boy he was trying to piece together.

Troy bristled at the remark. "A while," he muttered.

"I see. Still not goin' to tell us no more about yourself." He grinned menacingly. "You ashamed of your past, boy? Got somethin' to hide, maybe?"

Troy clenched and unclenched his fists and said nothing.

"Why don't ya leave the boy be, Toby? He's been through enough gawkin' fer one day."

"Sure, Pop. Sure. But I'd be careful hirin' me a boy I don't know nothin' about!"

"He's done an honest day's work. And he keeps his nose where it belongs, not stickin' it into other people's business like some folks I know!"

The intended insult reached its mark. The tailor drew himself up haughtily to his full, though short, stature as his face turned brilliantly red. He said nothing throughout the rest of the measuring process except to mumble to himself unintelligibly.

At last, the ordeal was over, and Jeremy and Troy were back in the cool, fragrant outdoors.

"Fresh air!" Jeremy exclaimed. "Why a tailor would smoke them awful cigars like he does is beyond me. It takes weeks to git the smell out of the clothes he makes!" He glanced over at Troy. "The man reminds me of a weasel."

Troy laughed at the comment. It was uplifting to laugh, something he hadn't been able to do in a long time.

CHAPTER 5

The Present

T roy was dead tired that night. The floor would be uncomfortable, but he was thankful for a place to sleep indoors. It was raining outside, and the pitter-patter of the drops against the roof overshadowing the store's front porch was a comforting sound to him. The window was open, and the rain-freshened air drifted through in bursts of sudden cool breezes.

Mary was asleep in the rocker. Troy didn't know if he could fall asleep like that—sitting in a chair. He wondered if it were easier for her because it reminded her of the platform rocker back home. She had loved that rocker. It was the one piece of furniture she still possessed after her husband, Colby, had left home—after they'd lost everything except the bare necessities of life. It was his mother's special oak chair with delicate flowers carved along the upper posts. Colby had ordered it from back east and given it to his wife as a wedding present. But this time, Mary had insisted they leave it behind. It could have fit into the wagon with the other supplies, but the memories it brought with it were too painful. Besides, they'd had little time to load the wagon; every second had counted.

Troy pictured his mother sitting in that chair while she mended, knitted, or read stories to him when he was little. For her sake, it would have been nice to have the chair since it was doubtful they'd ever be able to go back home or afford one like it again. Still, Troy was glad he didn't have the daily reminder of his father—of who he was and what he'd done.

He could hear Angie's steady but somewhat congested breathing and was grateful her fever had broken before the doctor arrived. Thankful she hadn't divulged anything incriminating, he sent a silent prayer of gratitude Heavenward.

Angie had never seen their father except for the picture of him in their mother's Bible. Troy hadn't seen much of his pa either, which was a blessing for himself and his mother. When Colby came home, he'd start drinking, leading to uncontrolled anger and violence. Troy had been the object of that anger many times. But Mary bore the brunt of the physical, verbal, and emotional abuse. It bothered Troy that he had never been brave or strong enough to protect his mother. But he had only been a child; what could he have done?

The only good memory he had of his father was from his sixth birthday—yet, even that day had been bittersweet.

As Troy lay down on a thick blanket on the floor, covering himself with another thick blanket, he thought back to that day.

Rolling over in his bed and rubbing his sleepy eyes, Troy lay quietly listening to the screeching cries of a giant hawk as it glided through the air directly above the house. Then, suddenly realizing the day's importance and impatient to enjoy it, he pushed the covers aside, scrambled to his knees, and threw open the shutters above his small wooden bed. Poking his head through the window, he called out brightly into the fragrant air. "Mornin', Mr. Hawk!" Noticing a slight humming noise to his right, he turned his head to watch the tiny bird whose wings fluttered so quickly he could hardly see them move. It was busily gathering nectar from the sunny yellow flowers his mother had told him were called Lantana. He observed some tumbleweeds dancing about on the ground outside the window, encircled by a swirling cloud of dust. He felt the warmth of the sun on his face. Drawing his head back inside, he sat on the edge of his bed, took off his nightshirt, replaced it with the shirt he'd draped over the bedpost the night before, and drew up his britches.

Mama had said he was almost a man, and they would make a trip to town to buy some penny candy for his birthday. Troy shivered with excitement. The last time he'd had candy had been two years earlier, when he'd turned four. Clara Marshall had given a birthday party for her son Rod and him since their birthdays were so close together. "Almost twins," she had called them. It was hard for him to understand what had happened since then—why his pa had left town, why they'd moved into the little house, why he couldn't play with Rod anymore, and why he had to wait two years for penny candy.

He entered the front room, which doubled as a kitchen and parlor, just as his mother came through the door. She was dressed in her best blue calico dress, the only nice dress she owned, her curly brunette hair neatly tied back at the nape with a blue ribbon. "You're wearing your Sunday Meeting dress, Mama. It ain't the Lord's day, is it?"

Mary Daniels lowered the bucket of well water onto the table and looked lovingly at her son. "No, dear, but it's a day belonging to someone very important!" She winked at him as she brushed a stray hair from her eyes.

Troy blushed. "You mean me, Mama?"

"I don't know anyone else so special, do you?"

"Does that mean you remembered my birthday?"

"Mm-hmm."

"Are we still going into town for that candy you promised?"

"We most certainly are, young man." She held out her arms and smiled as he ran over and threw himself into her embrace.

29

Hugging him tightly, Mary was thrilled by the affectionate love of her child—the small fingers curled around her neck, the gentle breathing of this sensitive creature who was a vital part of her. In one way, she wished this could be his last birthday—that he'd never grow up but always remain a little boy—hers to love and care for. Tears welled up in her eyes. She blinked them back quickly, berating herself for thinking selfishly. Troy was getting older; for his sake, she could not want it any other way. Besides, he was only six; they would still have many more years together.

Suddenly, Troy drew himself away from his mother's enfolding arms, straightened his shoulders, and gave her an earnest yet quizzical look. "Am I too old for hugging and stuff now, Mama?"

Mary repressed the urge to laugh. "No one grows too old for love, Troy," she responded tenderly, "but you are indeed growing up into a man, and a fine one at that."

He beamed proudly.

"A man must be strong and brave," she continued. "He must be honest, upright, and wise. And a man—a real man—must also be gentle and kind. He must know how to be respectful and loving." A far-away wistful look passed over her face. "You must become that kind of man, Troy."

"Better listen to your mama, boy," came a deep, easy-going voice from the open doorway.

Startled, Mary looked up quickly and met the gaze of the intruder. "Colby," she said, her voice catching in her throat and producing only a raspy whisper.

"Been a long time, ain't it, Mary?"

Trembling, Mary rose to her feet, self-consciously smoothing her skirt, and faced him.

He was tall and rugged, with handsome facial features, roguish, laughing brown eyes, and thick, wavy brown hair. A smile played on his lips, revealing a dimple in his left cheek.

"I—I wasn't expecting you," Mary muttered blankly, not knowing what else to say.

Colby laughed. "I can reckon why. A man that don't visit his family fer months on end can't expect no great homecomin.'"

"Then ..." She stared at the floor briefly, her cheeks blushing a deep pink. When she spoke, her voice was filled with dread softened with a hint of hope—the hope she always held in a corner of her heart—hope that he had changed. "You're coming to stay?"

The twinkle in his eyes flickered briefly, then extinguished; his voice iced over. "I didn't say that, Mary. I brung somethin' for the boy is all."

Troy backed away from him, remembering the last time this man came to visit. Troy could almost feel the sting of Colby's belt across his back. He could see the horrified look in his mother's eyes. He could hear the slaps she'd endured after begging the man not to hurt him. "You brought me somethin' for my birthday, mister?" he asked hesitantly.

"Mister? He's forgotten me that quickly, has he? Guess ya never talk about me none, do ya?"

"What would you have me tell him, Colby?" Mary said, against her better judgment. She might have faced retribution for her comment if Troy hadn't broken into the conversation.

"I know who you are. You're my pa—the man who drinks bad stuff then acts mean and makes Mama and me sad. You're the man in the picture—the picture in Mama's Bible. The one she prays for and cries over."

"Is that what she does?" Colby asked as he lowered himself into a crouched position to be at an equal height with his son. He glanced up at Mary with cold eyes, the smile on his face now a thin, unemotional line. "How touchin.'"

Mary sighed and turned her face away from him. He hadn't changed. Why would she have thought differently? He was the same selfish, mean-spirited man who'd walked out on his family.

Colby turned his attention back to Troy. "Come here, boy. I have a present for ya."

Troy's heart fluttered. A present, a real present—not just penny candy. Colby held out a long, slender box wrapped in brown paper that he'd kept hidden behind his back. Timidly, Troy took it, forgetting his fear of the man who was more like a stranger to him than his own flesh and blood. He sat on the floor, eagerly tore off the paper, and opened the box. It was a tin train like the one he'd seen at the General Store. Mama had said it came all the way from Philadelphia, a big town in the east, and that it cost lots of money—more than she could afford.

Troy lifted the train from the package and set it on the floor. "Look, Mama," he cried with delight, "it even has a coal car just like the one in Mr. Timbley's store!" He rolled it across the uneven plank floor. "And the wheels move, Mama! Look! The wheels move!"

Mary sighed. "It's wonderful," she remarked as she thought how her simple gift of penny candy paled in comparison.

Colby's eyes twinkled again with the cocky, self-assured sparkle that had captivated her as a young love-sick girl. Her eyes met his. Colby had won his son's affection with a simple toy. *Is that why he came home,* she mused, *to steal Troy away from me?*

Colby left soon afterward.

Enthralled with his new treasure, Troy was no longer interested in going to town.

Mary hid her suffocating hurt and raging emotions within her heart. She managed to smile at her son with his every utterance of glee. That night, she covered her pillow with tears. The penny candy would have to wait.

CHAPTER 6

Discussions

The rest of the first few weeks in Spring River passed by uneventfully. Troy was beginning to feel a part of the isolated town, almost like it had always been his home. He was also getting to know individual townspeople on a personal, friendly basis. The exception was Toby, who did remind him of a weasel.

Mary and Angie spent time with Tess or explored the surroundings they now called home. During the early evening, Mary often sat outside on the store's porch, a heavy shawl around her shoulders, knitting an afghan with the pretty shades of blue and green yarn Tess had given her. She secretly planned to give it to the Williams as a "thank you" for their kind hospitality.

"Wish I knew what was troublin' him, Tess," Jeremy remarked to his wife one night after supper once the Daniels had gone to their room. "He sure is carryin' a heap of burdens on them young shoulders."

"I know what ya mean. I admire him, though. I admire all of them. They got something that's helpin' them through the rough waters. Faith, she called it."

"Who called it?"

"Troy and Angie's mama, Mary. Such a sweet woman she is. It's a shame her husband passed away."

"She tell ya that?"

"What?"

"That her husband died." Jeremy reached for a biscuit before Tess had a chance to store it in the bread bin.

She slapped his hand playfully. "Don't ya think ya had enough of them at supper? Ya'll be makin' yerself sick."

"I can never git enough of yer biscuits."

"Oh, all right then. Go ahead."

"Don't mind if I do," he said, taking a big bite after adding a large pad of butter. "Back to what we was talkin' about. Did Mary tell ya her husband died?"

"No, but I reckon he did. Fact is, they never mention him at all."

"Troy told Toby that his father was alive. That's all he told him. The boy didn't want to say no more. Seems to me they's right ashamed of him."

"Oh, that Toby. I wouldn't tell him anythin' either. He's so, so—"

"Aggravatin'?"

"Yes. Anyway, I don't feel it's right to pry."

"I think Toby's done enough snoopin' fer the whole town! He comes in the store most every day and pesters Troy to tell him more about his past."

"Poor Troy. Can't help but feel sorry fer him." Tess shook her head sadly.

Jeremy nodded in agreement. "I sure hope things work out fer them here. I'd hate to lose him. He's a right good worker, jest like he promised he'd be. And I ain't all that easy to work fer."

"That's true, dear," Tess said slyly, her deep velvet green eyes twinkling.

"Now, woman, ya ain't got to agree with everythin' I say!"

"Pop, yer a crusty old man with a heart of gold." She gave him a squeeze.

"Don't go fussin' over me, either," he complained, vainly trying to conceal his enjoyment.

He got up from the table and sauntered over to his favorite chair. "Been spendin' a great deal of time with Mary, have ya? I seen her come through the store quite often and up the stairs, she and Angie."

Tess filled the washtub with water and began scrubbing the dishes. "Somewhat," she said, hoping he wouldn't ask much more. "We do our mendin' and such like together. Makes it a whole lot more interestin' havin' someone to talk to. She's workin' on a real pretty afghan with that yarn I give her."

"That Angie is very well-behaved, too. Dear little thing."

Jeremy was curious but didn't want to sound too anxious to know what their conversations were about. He had a sneaking suspicion but wanted to verify it without upsetting Tess. "What do ya talk about when yer sewin'?" he asked casually.

"Oh, different things."

Jeremy knew his wife well enough to sense she was holding something back. "Religion?"

"Sometimes," she said hesitantly, knowing her husband might not approve.

His suspicions confirmed, Jeremy grunted. "I was afeared of that. I told the boy he warn't to talk to me or my customers about his religion. I reckon he set his mama after ya."

Tess put her dishcloth on the table. "Jeremy, she warn't 'set after me.' What they believe is deep down. It ain't a religion with them. It's a regular part of their lives. It jest comes out naturally."

"Uh-huh. Ya—ya ain't becomin' religious yerself, is ya?"

"Well, I ... no."

"Good. I seen ya bow yer head afore supper tonight. Thought maybe ya was prayin' or somethin'."

"Well, I—I was, but I ain't got saved yet if that's what yer meanin'."

"Saved. Is that what they call it?"

"Yes."

"Hmph! Don't reckon we need to be saved from anythin'. What do ya think?"

Tess didn't answer. She was deep in thought about her sinful heart, death, and the hereafter. Those thoughts had plagued her for the last few days; they were subjects she didn't dare share with her husband. She knew why he didn't want to discuss it. He'd told her many times that he'd seen lots of hypocrites in his day—those who went to church and claimed to love God but lived just the opposite. He'd said he'd always been a good-living man, and when his time came, God would recognize that fact.

CHAPTER 7

Rachel

There were quite a few citizens of Spring River whom Troy had not met, including many of the local ranchers and their hands, the hotel manager, and the one who mattered most—the one who'd been out of town trying to chase down some rustlers. Troy hadn't given much thought to him until the day he appeared in the doorway of Mom and Pop's Mercantile. Though Troy knew he was innocent of the charge against him and had committed several verses to heart about fear, his legs felt like jelly as the muscular man with the shining silver badge strode into the room and extended his hand in greeting. "Hello, son. You must be Troy."

"Yes, sir," Troy answered despite his nervousness.

"I've heard a lot about you."

Troy felt a choking sensation in the back of his throat and a surge of dizziness. "You have, sir?" He wondered if the sheriff had talked to several townspeople to get his information or just Toby; Toby alone would have given him all there was to know. *Could news have traveled here from Tuscon?* Troy wondered.

The sheriff smiled. "Relax, son. It was all good." The tone of his voice changed. "Unless you have some reason to fear the law."

"No—no, sir," Troy stammered.

"Mark Kirby's the name."

Troy acknowledged him with a slight nod.

"Well, howdy, sheriff!" Jeremy cackled.

"Here, sir, let me get that for you." Troy took the heavy bundle of flour Jeremy had brought from the storage room and set it under the window next to the sugar.

"Thank ya, Troy," Jeremy said, then turned his attention back to the sheriff. "Ya met my new helper?"

"Yes. Yes, I have."

"Fine boy, sheriff. A hard worker."

"So I've heard!"

"Which reminds me, Troy," Jeremy interjected, "the stagecoach is due any time now. There should be lots of boxes on it fer us, so I reckon Lonnie will be stoppin' right outside the shop."

Eager to leave the conversation, Troy responded enthusiastically, "I'll go out right away, sir, so I can unload them as soon as the stage arrives."

Mark watched Troy as he left. His voice took on an air of suspicion. "What do you know about him, Pop?"

Jeremy lowered his voice in case Mary and Angie could hear. "Not much. Mighty secretive fellow. Real religious. Nice family. Why? Ya heard somethin'?"

"No. No, I was just wondering. It seems strange for a whole family to show up out of nowhere—not mentioning any specific place they came from, not talking about their past. Toby seems to think there's something more to their story—something questionable. But, I guess if they aren't causing any trouble, there's no need to get all excited about it, is there?"

"Hmph! Toby!"

Mark laughed. "He's in the height of his glory trying to find out the particulars on the outsiders."

"It's about to drive him crazy!" Jeremy chuckled. "And the boy there—he ain't about to give Toby's curiosity no satisfaction."

"Well, if you run into any trouble with him, Pop, don't hesitate to let me know." Mark clapped the shopkeeper good-naturedly on the shoulder and left.

Troy watched as the sheriff walked to his office. Relieved, he searched his mind to see if he had told the truth to the man—that he didn't have a reason to fear the law. *It's not the law I'm concerned about,* Troy reassured himself. *It's Rod.*

Mark had been genuinely impressed with the newcomer. However, despite that, he decided to look through the stack of wanted posters that had piled up on his desk as soon as possible. For the moment, he was locking up the jail and heading home for a long-needed rest. It had been a grueling and disappointing three weeks in the saddle without finding the men involved in rustling from some of the local herds.

Troy waited on the porch for the stage, which, as usual, was late. When it finally stopped, Troy greeted the driver and signed for the boxes. As he stacked the parcels in front of the mercantile, he mentally noted how he could carry them into the store with the least number of trips.

"Oh, excuse me, ma'am," he apologized as he accidentally brushed against one of the disembarking passengers. It startled, thrilled, and frightened Troy when he looked up and saw the pretty face with the slightly upturned nose, blue eyes, and long golden locks of hair cascading past her shoulders.

"Tr—"

"Shh," he whispered hoarsely. "Act like you don't know me."

Rachel nodded. "Apology accepted, sir. No harm done," she replied.

"Troy, I'm runnin' extra late tonight," Lonnie said as he and Troy untied the last wooden crates from the rack on top of the stage and set them on the porch. "I need to make it over to Cedar Ridge by nightfall. Would you mind helpin' with this young lady's luggage and seein' her over to the hotel?" Lonnie tossed the passenger's two carpetbags to Troy, assuming he'd take the responsibility.

"Not at all," Troy said.

Lonnie, already back up in his seat, nodded to him, cracked the whip above the horses' heads, and continued his journey.

Troy opened the door to the store and peered inside. Jeremy was wiping off the candy jars on the counter while mumbling about children's sticky fingers. "Pop, Lonnie asked me to walk one of his passengers over to the hotel. All right with you if I do that before bringing in the boxes?"

"Fine by me. Jest make sure them boxes ain't in the way of customers tryin' to git into the store."

"Yes, sir. Will do!" Troy maneuvered a few crates to a safe place under the window, then picked up the two carpetbags.

"Rachel," he said under his breath as they crossed the street. "Meet me behind the church tonight after dark."

"Troy I—"

"Don't say any more for now. It ain't safe," he warned as they reached the boardwalk. "And remember, you don't know me."

"You want me to lie?"

"Course not. Just don't make it obvious that we know each other."

The two walked in silence until they arrived at the hotel.

"Is it all right to leave these with the desk clerk, ma'am?" Troy said loudly. "I'm sure he'll be more than happy to take them to your room. I need to get back to my job."

"Yes. Yes, sir, that would be fine," she answered, feeling foolish for treating her fiancé as though he were a stranger.

Troy opened the door for her, took her bags inside, and set them down by the front desk. "Excuse me, sir, could you see this lady's bags get to her room?"

"Of course," the clerk with the wire-rimmed spectacles and receding hairline said cheerfully.

Troy waited until it was dark, then told his mother he was going for a walk. Not wanting to upset her, he didn't mention anything about Rachel.

40

Meandering slowly behind the town's buildings to get to the church, he carefully peered around each corner before proceeding. The saloon was filled with cowhands. Troy guessed they would keep the sheriff busy enough to allow him some private time to speak with Rachel.

He paced back and forth until he saw her in the moonlight—moonlight far too bright for comfort. "Rachel, why did you come to Spring River?" he scolded.

"I had to see you, Troy."

"How did you know we were here?"

"I guessed. You told me a while ago that you'd like to move here someday to be far away from your pa."

"It would have been best for you not to follow us."

"Almost two months have gone by, Troy. I had to see you—to know you were all right."

"I will be until Rod gets here!"

"How could he have followed me? I haven't given my name out anywhere."

"The coach lines will have a record!"

Rachel hung her head sadly. "I'm—I'm sorry, Troy. I didn't think about that. Aren't you even the least bit glad to see me?" she asked, a hurt look on her face.

"Oh, Rachel ..." He cupped her face in his hands and looked directly into her eyes. "You don't know how much I've wanted to see you—how much I've missed you! I think about you all the time, but it's just not safe now. You'll have to leave on tomorrow's stage."

"What? Troy, I've come all this way!"

"There's a busybody here that's probably spying on us at this minute!"

"Oh?" she said unbelievingly.

"I'm serious, Rachel. He knows what's happening around town before it happens. He's been asking questions."

"Does he have any idea?"

41

"I don't think so. But if you meet up with anyone before the stage leaves, you can't let on that you know me. Otherwise, folks will bombard you with questions. The truth is bound to come out."

"You're not afraid of the truth, are you, Troy?"

"Of course not, but—I have no witnesses, Rachel. None except for Pa, and even if I knew where he was, even if he came here, what good would that do? Don't you see? If any of the story gets out—any of it, I don't stand a chance."

"Oh, Troy, I feel so sorry for you. I want so much to help you."

"You can—by leaving. Look, all I need is some time to start a new life, to make a new name for myself—an honest, upright name that ain't tainted by my pa's reputation. When that happens, Rachel—when I can stand on my own two feet. When folks respect me—then I'll send for you. I promise."

"I hate this!" she exclaimed.

"So do I, but it's the only choice we have right now. Rod's sure to follow you here. If you go tomorrow and travel to a few more towns, maybe he'll think you're still looking for me. Please, Rachel, you have to understand. This is my family's chance for a new start."

Tears formed in Rachel's eyes and escaped down her cheeks. "And us, Troy? What about us? What about our chance for a new start? We were going to be married!"

"You can't marry a dead man, Rachel. I have to clear my name first."

"How?"

Troy shook his head. "I don't know. If Rod finds me, I may not have the chance."

"Oh, Troy." She wrapped her arms around him and snuggled against his chest, the tears flowing freely. "I'm so sorry! I may have put your life in danger. Please, please forgive me."

"It's all right," he said soothingly, then suddenly pulled away from her. "What about your father? How did you convince him to let you come?"

"I have a cousin in Spring River. I asked Father if I could visit her. Her family owns one of the nearby ranches. They're supposed to come into town for me tomorrow."

"A cousin? A cousin who lives here?" Troy ran his fingers nervously back through his hair. "What are the chances?" he mumbled to himself before questioning Rachel. "Does she know about us?"

"I—I don't know." She paused for a moment, then added sheepishly. "Jill may have been invited to the wedding."

He took her hands in his. "That's all the more reason why you need to leave—before she realizes who I am. Besides, don't you think your father will figure out why you really came to Spring River? Don't you think he'll assume I'm here?"

"I don't think he'll say anything to Rod if that's what you're worried about."

"Your father approved our engagement because he wanted you to be happy. But he's never been keen on us getting married. Now, after everything that's happened, he probably hates me. Please, Rachel. You have to leave—not just for my sake, but for Angie and Mama."

"How are they? I've been thinking about them and praying for them."

"Then your prayers have been answered." Troy relaxed a little with the change of subject. "Angie was sick when we first arrived. She got delirious and came close to giving me away. But she's fine now. Mama's doing as well as can be expected under the circumstances. The Lord's brought her through so much already. Somehow, she'll get through this, too."

"So, you're working at that store where I got off the stage?"

"Yes. It's a good job. We've got a room to live in, plenty to eat. But if your cousin finds out who we are ..."

A gust of wind swept around the corner of the church. They both shuddered.

"I should have worn my shawl. It's getting chilly!"

Troy drew Rachel into his embrace. "Does that help?"

She looked up at him and grinned. "Absolutely!"

43

"Oh, Rachel, I love you so much, but I can't take a chance on someone seeing us together. I—I probably won't see you again before you leave. Please try to understand. There will be a time for us, Rachel. Just—not now."

"It seems like the wait will be forever."

"I know."

Reluctantly, she pulled herself away.

Troy reached for her hand, brought it to his lips, and kissed it. "I love you, Rachel. No matter what happens, I want you always to remember that."

She stared at his handsome face—the strong lines and square jaw, dark hair, and deep brown eyes—as if trying to tuck away each feature in her heart. "And I'll always love you, Troy—no matter what happens."

CHAPTER 8

Rod

Troy tried to stifle the tense, apprehensive feeling that crept over him the following day. He encouraged himself, thinking that all would be well if no one had seen him talking to Rachel. However, if her cousin, Jill, entered the store, which, he reasoned, had probably already occurred, it could only be a matter of time before she realized who he was. And, if Jill knew Rachel was coming for a visit, she would wonder why she had gone back home. Either way, whether Rachel left or stayed, Troy knew he would need to talk with his mother as soon as possible about moving away from Spring River—a conversation he was dreading almost as much as the move itself. *How will I explain it to Pop?* Clumsily, his hands trembling, he stocked the shelves with the goods that had arrived on the stage the day before.

His uneasiness did not escape Jeremy's keen observation. "What's got into ya, boy?"

"W—what do you mean, sir?"

"Why yer as jumpy as a three-horned toad!"

"I—I'm sorry, sir."

"Don't be sorry. Don't bother me none, 'less'n ya was to drop some of them things yer stackin'. Somethin' troublin' ya?"

"It's—it's nothing, sir."

"Hmph! In other words, mind my own business, huh?"

"I didn't mean that, sir. I—"

Jeremy laughed. "Now I know what ya meant. I shouldn't have been pryin'. I detest it in other folks. Guess I ought to dislike it in myself." He sauntered off to the back room while Troy continued to arrange the sundry items.

"Mornin', Troy," Toby's squeaky voice sounded behind him.

Startled, Troy dropped the three cans in his hands. "Good morning, Mr. Jenson," he answered in a polite but irritated voice as he bent down to pick them up.

"I noticed you was in the company of a young lady last evening."

Troy looked at him disbelievingly. "You don't miss a thing, do you?"

"What's that, boy?"

Troy shook his head. "Nothing, sir." He checked the cans for dents before arranging them on the shelf.

"Friend of yours from back home, is she?"

Jeremy came out of the storage area whistling a tune that ended when he saw Toby.

Troy quickly went to his employer's side. "Is there anything else you'd like me to do, sir?"

Toby followed him. "You're changin' the subject, boy."

"You're right," Troy muttered under his breath.

Jeremy was angry. "This here store ain't open yet, Toby."

"He's hidin' somethin' from you, Pop."

"Toby, ain't ya ever gonna learn not to be busybodyin' in other people's affairs! Now go on, git!" Jeremy said impatiently.

"All right, Pop. But I'm warnin' you. There's a shiftiness about that boy. I'm tellin' you he's runnin' from somethin'."

"Better listen to him, old man. He's right."

Troy recognized the voice instantly. He spun around. "Rod!"

"What's the matter, Daniels?" Rod exclaimed. "You look as though you've seen a ghost."

Ever since it had become common knowledge that Colby was an outlaw, Rod only referred to Troy by his last name.

As Rod moved closer to him, Troy instinctively backed up. "How—how did you find me?"

"I'll admit it was hard. You were clever, brushing away your tracks in hopes we'd take the wrong path. But it was all in vain," Rod taunted. "As fate would have it, your fiancée gave you away."

Toby had stood in stunned silence when the stranger entered the door, but now his curiosity got the best of him. "What's goin' on?" he asked excitedly. "What's goin' on?"

Both Troy and Rod ignored him.

"Who else is with you?" Troy's voice shook. His heart pulsated violently against his chest.

"Scared, aren't you, Daniels?" Rod taunted him.

"Why can't you just leave me alone?"

"I think you know the reason for that!"

"What's goin' on?" Toby was shivering with delight. But he was also a little fearful and shuffled sideways until he stood close to Jeremy.

"I'm innocent!" Troy said to Rod.

"If you were innocent, you wouldn't have run away!"

"You didn't leave me any choice!"

Rod drew his gun from its holster.

Toby let out a yelp and ran behind Jeremy for protection.

"Hoping to get Rachel out of town before I found you?" Rod asked as he pointed the gun at Troy.

Toby peeked out from his hiding place just long enough to question Troy. "Rachel. Is that the name of the girl you was talkin' to?"

Jeremy looked over his shoulder at the shaking tailor, gave him a disgusted look, then turned back to Rod. "Now look here, young man," he said boldly, pointing a long slender finger at him. "I don't take kindly to someone bustin' into my store and pullin' a gun on my hired help."

47

"Maybe you should have found out more about your help before you hired him."

Toby felt a little more courageous. He peered around Jeremy again. "He's runnin' from the law, ain't he?"

"His whole family's running from the law."

Delighted to learn his assessment had been correct, Toby proudly stepped out from behind his human shield. "I knew it! I knew it!"

"That ain't true! I—"

"Ever hear of Colby Daniels?" Rod asked, cutting off Troy's defense.

"Daniels! Daniels!" Toby repeated. "Colby Daniels! I knew I'd heard that name before!"

Jeremy squinted his eyes and looked down over the rim of his glasses. His face scrunched up into a scowl at the mention of the outlaw. "Ya ain't meanin'—Killer Colby?"

"That's right. Killer Colby. He's Troy's pa."

Toby's mouth gaped open; his eyes bulged.

Jeremy shook his head sadly. "That true, son? Killer Colby's your pa?"

Troy hung his head. It was over; he couldn't hide the fact any longer. "Yes, sir," he answered quietly.

"Why didn't ya tell me, Troy?" the old man asked gently.

"Would you have hired me if I did? Would anyone have hired me?"

Jeremy came to Troy's defense. "A body ain't got no chance to be pickin' out who's to be their pa," he said to Rod. "I don't see how he should be held responsible fer what his pa's done."

"You think he should be accountable for what he's done?" Rod queried.

Jeremy couldn't imagine that the young man he'd come to admire and appreciate could be capable of any crime. "Such as—"

"Murder!" Rod replied, glaring at Troy.

"Murder!" Toby shrieked. His stomach started quivering when he realized he'd been face-to-face for weeks with a murderer! He gasped and ran behind Jeremy again, this time to protect himself from Troy.

Troy raised his eyes and looked directly at his employer. "I was already brought to trial," he said, speaking passionately yet keeping his voice as low as possible. He was thankful Mary and Angie were upstairs helping Mom clean up the breakfast dishes, but he didn't want to take a chance on them overhearing the conversation. "The jury couldn't decide—the judge declared it a mistrial!"

"That's because you were tried in a town where your Mama grew up, and everyone knew you since you were a little boy. Some of the jurors were biased. They just felt sorry for you," Rod sputtered contemptuously.

"That's not True! It's not true, Pop. I'm innocent! I never hurt anyone in my life!"

"There was talk of a new trial," Rod added. "The sheriff made the mistake of letting Troy go home instead of back to jail. Then he ran. If that doesn't prove his guilt, I don't know what does!"

Toby peered around Jeremy again and stared at Troy. "A murderer!"

Troy lost his temper with Toby. "You want to see a murderer? You ask him," he said, gesturing towards Rod. "Ask him how he tried to have me lynched! You ask him!"

Then, to Jeremy, he added, "If the sheriff hadn't come along at the right moment, I'd be dead. I—I pleaded with the sheriff to lock me up for my protection. Instead, he told me it would be better if I left town." He nodded his head toward Rod. "We both knew he'd try again to hang me before I could ever make it to a second trial!"

Jeremy took a few steps toward Troy and gently put his hand on the boy's shoulder. With his bodyguard gone, Toby ran and hid behind the cracker barrel.

"Calm down, son," Jeremy said softly. "Everythin's gonna be all right."

"Everything's going to be made right," Rod stated emphatically, "because I'm taking you to the sheriff in this town, Daniels. I'll see to it that you stand trial here, where no one really knows you—where the truth can come out once and for all. Besides, I've got new evidence that will put you where you belong—at the end of a rope!"

Troy was concerned. "What evidence?"

"You'll find out soon enough." Rod cocked his gun and motioned for Troy to move. Troy sighed deeply and walked slowly toward the door just as the sheriff entered the shop.

On seeing Rod's gun drawn, he drew his own. "What's going on here?"

"I was bringing this criminal to you, sheriff," Rod answered.

"I didn't do anything, sheriff. That's the truth."

"He's a liar!" Rod insisted. "He murdered my little sister!"

There were times when Mark didn't like his job; this was one of them. "I'm sorry, son," he said to Troy. "I'd like to believe you, but ..." He put his revolver in its holster, reached into his pocket, and retrieved a folded piece of paper. "I found this in my mail pile." He unfolded the paper with Troy's image and held it up for all to see. "I have no choice. Troy Daniels, you're under arrest for the murder of Jessica Marshall."

Troy stared in disbelief at the wanted poster. The knot in his stomach rose to his throat as if it would choke him. His first reaction was to fight back, not just at Rod or the sheriff, though he knew the man was just doing his duty, but at his father and all the heartbreak he'd caused through the years. Clenching his jaw and tensing his muscles, he flexed his fists, then let his hands hang free, and his shoulders sag. Resigning himself to his fate, he meekly turned around and put his hands behind his back for the sheriff to cuff him.

He spoke to Jeremy just before leaving the shop. "Will you—will you tell Mama what's happened?"

"Of course, son."

Rod holstered his gun and walked beside Troy and the sheriff.

Now that he knew he was out of danger, Toby followed close behind, feeling enormously proud of himself for his part in capturing the son of a notorious outlaw—and a murderer, at that! "I'll be willin' to testify! I knew all along he was hidin' somethin'!"

Though Troy kept his head down, he could feel the stares of those around him—people beginning their outside chores gathering water from the well or sweeping porches, and early shoppers chatting with one another. He heard a few windows being raised as Toby hollered as loud as he could on the way to the sheriff's office while pointing his stubby index finger at Troy, "He's a murderer! He's a murderer!"

Jeremy watched them until they disappeared into the sheriff's office, then trudged wearily up the back stairs to deliver the news.

CHAPTER 9

A Secret Revealed

Troy sat on the rough wooden bed with its thin worn-out mattress and forlornly surveyed his surroundings. Leaning back against the thick cement wall, he ran his fingers through his hair and shook his head in defeat. *This is it,* he thought grimly. *There's no getting out of it this time.* A sudden overwhelming emptiness surged through him; he felt alone—totally alone in the world. He glanced up at the ceiling and spoke through it to the gates of Heaven. "I've got no one to help me, Lord. No one but You. It will take a miracle."

The large, heavy door between the sheriff's office and the room housing a narrow hallway and two cells squeaked open. "Take as long as you need, ma'am," Mark said to Mary as he unlocked the door to Troy's cell.

"Thank you, sheriff. That's very kind of you."

"You're welcome." Mark locked the cell behind her and returned to his desk.

Mary placed the tray of food she'd brought on top of the tall wooden crate in the corner that served as a table. "I brought you some breakfast, Troy," she said.

Troy rose, crossed to the window, laced his fingers around the cold bars, then gazed blankly at the street. "I'm not hungry."

"You must eat something," she said. "I brought you the Bible. I thought it might bring you some comfort."

Troy turned toward her and held out his arms. She walked into his embrace and sobbed on his shoulder.

"Mama," he said brokenly, "I'm sorry. I'm so sorry."

Mary held him at arm's length, searching his eyes with her own. "What do you mean, 'sorry,' Troy? You haven't done anything."

"I brought you more sorrow. You don't deserve any of this. You deserve to live in a fine house with a respectable name and children you can be proud of."

"I am proud of my children. Both of them."

She turned away from him, took the handkerchief she had stuffed into the waistband of her skirt, and wiped her eyes. "Troy, I have something to tell you—something I think you should know."

"What is it? Did something happen to Angie, Rachel?"

"Rachel?"

"She's in town. I was going to tell you, but—"

"Does Rachel know you're in jail?"

"I don't know. I just spoke to her last night."

Mary sat on the side of the bed and began weeping again.

"Mama—is it Angie? Is she all right?"

Mary nodded her head. "She's fine. It's about me, Troy."

Troy sat down beside her. "What is it, Mama?"

"It's *my* fault you're in here. The troubles I've had are *my* fault. It's because of *me* that you and Angie have had such a hard life."

"How can you say that?" he asked as he tenderly placed his strong right arm around her shaking shoulders and drew her close. "Pa's the one who caused all the problems, Mama, not you."

"But it's *my* fault he ended up being your pa."

"Oh, Mama, please don't blame yourself."

Mary rested her head on his shoulder. Troy had always been such a comfort, such a blessing to her. "You never knew your grandma or grandpa. I haven't talked much about them because I've felt so guilty. They were wonderful people. I was blessed to have them as my parents. Only I didn't realize how fortunate I was."

Mary nervously bit down on her lower lip, trying to keep it from trembling, then continued. "I gave my heart to Christ when I was just a little girl. But, as I got older, I decided I didn't like my parents' strict ways. I wanted to know more about the world and thought I knew better than they did. Then I met your pa. I was so young, just sixteen, when we met. He was tall and handsome; you look so much like he did when he was younger."

"Like the picture you keep in your Bible?"

"Yes. Like the picture. I always felt special when I was near Colby. He knew how to sweet-talk me into falling for him. I knew he wasn't a Christian and that God forbade me to marry him. My mother and father warned me, but I was stubborn and willful. I thought I knew best. I thought I loved Colby. Besides, I wanted to get away from home to be free to do as I pleased. So I ran away, and we got married."

Mary paused momentarily, thinking how different her life might have turned out if she hadn't been so impetuous and bent on having her own way. She lifted her head and turned her tear-stained face toward her son. "Oh, Troy, don't you see? If I hadn't disobeyed God and my parents, you wouldn't be in such a desperate situation. You might have grown up in a fine house. You might have had a reputable name and a father who loved you. It's all my fault!" Tears spilled down her cheeks once more.

"Mama," Troy said consolingly. "Mama, whatever happened in the past is past. You can't change it now. You can't live in a world of 'what if' or 'if only.' What's done is done. Have you asked God to forgive you?"

"Yes, but I never had the chance to ask my parents to forgive me. It's one of the deepest regrets I have. Almost seven years passed before I discovered how your pa had gotten his money. By then, I received word that my parents were with the Lord." She stared blankly in front of her, not focusing on anything. "I never had the chance to say, 'I'm sorry.' I know the Lord has forgiven me. I guess sometimes I have a hard time forgiving myself. And now, with what's happening to you—"

"Please, Mama, put it behind you. I'm not blaming you. I've got to believe God is still in control. You need to believe that, too."

"It will take a miracle, Troy—a miracle for you to be found innocent."

Troy drew in a deep breath and let it out slowly. "I know."

Mary wiped the remaining tears from her eyes and allowed Troy to help her to her feet. "I needed to tell you, Troy. I've held it in all this time."

"It's over now, Mama. You're forgiven."

She nodded. "Yes, forgiven. If only we humans could fully grasp the meaning of that word. I have so much to be thankful for. The Lord has protected you from Rod so far. He's provided us with food and shelter. My children both know Jesus as their Savior." She paused, then added thoughtfully. "Perhaps, one day, your pa will come to know Him." There was a faint glimmer of expectancy in her brown eyes. "I can hope, can't I, Troy?"

"Yes, Mama, you can hope," Troy agreed, although his heart was far from wishing anything good for his father.

Mary smiled at her son. No matter what happened, she was proud of him—very proud. She gave Troy a parting hug, holding him tighter and longer than usual—afraid to let go, afraid it might be the last time.

CHAPTER 10

Remembering

It was dark. A thin ray of light shone through the cell window onto the page of Scripture Troy was attempting to read in the dimness. Mary had returned at lunch and supper to take back the empty food tray and bring him more to eat. His appetite had returned, and he'd finished everything. Now, bedded down as comfortably as possible, lying between the softness of the two blankets his mother had supplied, he endeavored to encourage himself with God's Word.

Mark decided to spend the night in his office, rifle nearby, in case Rod paid an unplanned visit. He also thought that news about Troy's capture and impending trial might spread to surrounding towns. Since Spring River would have more to deal with than the sleepy little town could ever imagine if Colby got wind of his son's incarceration, Mark had written a list of men to deputize come morning.

"I'm going to be on the other side of that door," he told Troy, motioning to the thick wooden barrier between his office and the jail. "If you need anything, you just holler. You understand, boy?"

"Yes, sir," Troy responded as he closed the Bible; it was difficult to see the small print—better to wait until daylight. He rose from his bed and stood behind the cell door. "I'm sorry you have to deal with this, sheriff. I was hoping the trouble wouldn't follow us—hoping we could start a new life. Guess I didn't think about how us being here would affect everyone else if—"

"You have any idea where your pa might be?"

"No, sir. I haven't seen him since the night of the—"

"Murder?"

"Yes, sir."

"Then you *were* with him."

"Yes, sir—but I didn't hurt anyone."

"Why did you do it, son? Why did you go with him? You must have known he would be up to no good."

"I wasn't given a choice. There were four others besides my pa."

"They forced you to go, did they?" Mark rubbed his hand nervously across his chin.

"Yes, sir."

Mark hoped Troy was telling the truth about his innocence; he didn't want to be the one to carry out the boy's death sentence should he be lying and found guilty.

Troy had given his mother comfort and assurance on her visits—promises that all would be well. But later that evening, after he was confident from the snoring in the next room that the sheriff was asleep, he got up and restlessly paced back and forth across the six-by-nine-foot space, mentally reliving the night his pa had come for him.

"Troy," Mary said, laying her knitting aside as the sound of horses' hooves drew closer, then stopped in front of the little shack she and her children called home. "Troy, get the gun. I don't know what's going on, but ..." Rather than finish her sentence, Mary rose quickly from her chair and bolted the door.

His heart thumping wildly against his chest, Troy took the rifle from its rack above the fireplace and stood at the ready several feet from the door.

The sound of men's voices could be heard talking among themselves in slurred speech—the result of too much whiskey. One, in particular, stood out.

Mary gasped. "It's your pa!"

"Troy!" the gravelly voice bellowed. "Come out here, boy!"

Mary and Troy exchanged nervous glances. Troy knew his mother had feared such a day would come. They had even made emergency escape plans, but now that the time to implement them was here, they stood motionless as if frozen in place.

"Mama," Troy said in a steady voice, not wanting her to know how scared he was. "Go into the back room with Angie."

"I can't leave you here to face him alone, Troy."

"There's nothing you can do, Mama. Please—for Angie's sake."

Mary put her hand on her son's arm. "I love you, son. I'll be praying for you."

Troy nodded as Mary disappeared into the back room where her daughter lay peacefully asleep, oblivious to the night's danger.

"What do you want with me, Pa?" Troy shouted with as much courage as he could muster.

"I want ya to come with me." The door rattled as Colby tried to force it open. "Unbolt this, boy."

"No, Pa. Please—go away and leave us alone."

The door shook as Colby impatiently pounded on it. "I'm comin' in after ya!"

"I've got a gun, Pa." Troy breathed heavily, fear coursing through his body. His hands felt sweaty, the gun heavy.

There was an awkward stillness outside except for the sound of feet and whispered words. The next thing Troy knew, his father and two other men crashed through the door, splintering it into pieces. Troy stood in stunned silence.

"Ya gonna shoot me, boy? Ya gonna shoot yer own pa?" Colby questioned.

Troy cocked the rifle. "You're no pa to me," he stated boldly. "Now, take your men and go!"

"Ain't he the one to be givin' orders?" Colby said to his men. A sly smile crossed his handsomely rugged face, revealing the dimple in his left cheek and accentuating the scar proceeding from his chin to his left ear. "Where's yer ma, boy? And that sister of yers? I heard I had me a daughter. I'd like to see what she looks like."

Troy took several faltering steps backward until he stood flat against the door to the bedroom—all the while keeping his gun trained on his father. Colby glanced at his two henchmen, nodding toward each with a coded command to flank Troy, one on the left and the other on the right. Troy swallowed hard and nervously eyed the three outlaws surrounding him. He didn't stand a chance. He was outnumbered; from all indications, there were more outside. He would have to sacrifice himself for his mother and Angie.

"All right, Pa," Troy agreed, "I'll come with you. But, please, promise me nothing will happen to Mama and Angie."

"Sure, son. I jest need yer help with a little job me and the boys are goin' to pull off tonight. That's all. Besides, it's about time ya untie yerself from yer mother's apron strings. About time ya became a man."

Troy had no desire to be a man if it meant being like his pa, but he had no choice except to lower his rifle and follow them outside. He laid the gun on the floor; his mother might need it, and he didn't want to go armed to whatever his father was planning lest he be blamed if any shooting occurred.

Troy pictured himself riding off with them into the night. Over and over, he rehearsed the beginning moments of that ill-fated night. But the horror that happened later he purposely blocked from his thoughts. He would not—could not—allow himself to dwell on that!

Doubts, fear, and resentment flooded his mind. *It's not fair,* he told himself. *I don't deserve any of this! Mama and Angie don't deserve it, either, in spite of what Mama said. It's Pa who made our lives miserable all these years. It's Pa who made Mama work so hard to make ends meet. It's Pa who made me miss schooling because I had to help pay the bills. It's Pa who gave me a bad name. It's Pa who shot Jessica!*

He stopped in front of the small window, took hold of the steel bars, and gazed into the black darkness. *Where are you, Pa? Why am I in here, and you're out there? I'm innocent! And I—I can't pray for your salvation like Mama can! I don't care about your soul! You deserve punishment now and—and forever! I'm innocent! You're guilty! Why must I take your place?*

Immediately, conviction struck his heart. That's what Someone else had done for him—taken his place—the Innocent for the guilty. He sank to his knees on the cold stone floor. *Forgive me, Lord,* his heart cried out. *Forgive me! I don't understand why all this had to happen. I don't understand why I had to have Colby Daniels for a father, why I had to be forced to have a part in the break-in at Rob's house, why I was the one who got caught—the one who looked guilty. Don't let me blame You for it. Help me remember that behind all of this—this mess, You have a perfect plan.*

"Lord, I'm scared!" he whispered aloud. "I could be dead within a few weeks, maybe less. It's not that I'm afraid of what will happen to me after I die. I know I'll be with You. It's dying itself. It's being up on that scaffold with everyone watching while the noose is put around my neck." He put his hand up to his throat. A chill shot through his body as he remembered the fearful night after his trial when Rod had come for him. The night he'd looked death in the face.

"I come for 'justice,' Daniels!" Rod bellowed as the angry mob echoed the word.

Troy had come outside the house and closed the door behind him. He didn't want his mother or sister to see what was happening, even though he knew they could hear every word. "I already had a trial, Rod."

"You already had a trial, but justice wasn't done!"

"I'm innocent!"

"You're as innocent as your pa!" Rod retorted. There were nods and angry assents.

"Rod, please. Go home and leave me, my mama, and sister in peace."

"At least you still have a sister! Because of you, mine's gone! Maybe you should find out what it's like to have your sister shot dead!"

"Nobody touches Angie!" Troy threatened, even though he knew he couldn't defend her against so many. "Look, Rod. I'm as sorry as I can be about Jessica. But—I didn't do it! I didn't even have a gun with me!"

"You've got no proof of that, Daniels!"

Troy shook his head, then looked at Rod. "We were the best of friends, Rod." He scanned the crowd. "All of you—all of you were our friends at one time. Up until Pa ... Now you want nothing to do with us. You're ready to believe anything you hear—whether it's true or not."

A few men lowered their eyes, some exchanged glances, and others cursed under their breath. They all knew it was true. Through the years, the town had been divided in their treatment of Mary and her children—all because of Colby. Now, the town was divided again—this time about Troy's guilt or innocence.

Troy turned around to go back inside the house. When he did, Rod gave the signal. Several men rushed forward, grabbing Troy's arms and pinning them behind him. He felt the rope cut into his wrists as they were securely tied together. A cloth was put in his mouth and fastened behind his head. His legs felt weak and shaky as he was pushed through the crowd toward the road. He knew where they were taking him—to the hanging tree—the large oak on the outskirts of town. Though he had no hope of freeing himself, he tensed every muscle in his body, pushing back against his captors. Sweat broke out on his forehead despite the coolness of the air. He wanted to run his tongue over his suddenly parched lips but couldn't because of the choking cloth that pulled tightly against the corners of his mouth. *If only the sheriff would show up,* he thought. *But it's the middle of the night. No chance of that happening. Lord,* he prayed, *you're my only hope! Please—You were there! You know I'm innocent!*

By the time they came to the tree, Troy's legs buckled under him. A noose was placed around his neck; he felt it tighten enough to sense the rough prickly fibers rubbing against his skin. He swallowed hard and closed his eyes as strong arms lifted him onto a horse. The other end of the rope was thrown into the air over a thick branch. Troy took a deep breath through his nose of the musty, misty night air. Holding it for what seemed like hours, he anxiously anticipated the moment of death. He tried focusing his troubled mind on the glory that would be his when the ordeal was over—of waking up in Heaven and seeing Christ.

The rope missed its mark and fell to the ground. The mob muttered their disappointment as Troy released the air he'd been holding inside, his chest heaving, his heart thumping wildly.

"Try again," he heard Rod say. "This time, don't miss!"

"All right. All right. Don't worry." Troy recognized the grumbling voice of the man who ran the livery.

Troy took another deep breath.

"Stop right there!" the commanding voice of Sheriff Wilson thundered. "Drop the rope and get him down! Now!"

"We're just seeing that justice is done, sheriff!" Rod retorted.

"Now! Unless you want to join him at your own hanging party!"

Troy was lowered from the horse, then collapsed. Mary rushed over to him, stumbling past the men who were leaving as quickly as possible, hats down over their heads, hoping the sheriff wouldn't recognize them and hold them responsible for their actions.

"Mama—how?" Troy asked as he tried sitting up.

"Shh," Mary said as she gently untied his hands and removed the gag. "Just lie still, Troy."

"But how?"

"While you were talking with Pa, Mama and I crawled out the back window and ran to fetch the sheriff," Angie told him.

A trial, a near-lynching, and now another trial. Waiting in a lonely cell, Troy was about to face the false accusations a third time. And maybe things wouldn't end as well. "Oh, Lord," he said, continuing his prayer. "It's Mama and Angie bearing the brunt of ..." His voice trailed off as he thought of his beloved mother and little sister being left alone. "And Rachel—Rachel! She'll be a widow before she's even married."

"I'm scared, Lord. I know You delivered me before, but there's no way out this time. There's nothing I can do! I don't have any witnesses except—except You.

"And I—I still don't think I can pray for my father's soul. I don't care about him!"

Troy remembered the verse he had read earlier: '*And David encouraged himself in the Lord.*' "Oh, dear Heavenly Father," he cried, "Encourage me. Encourage me!"

CHAPTER 11

A Time for Us

T he following day, it was raining so hard that drops splashed through the cell window. Troy welcomed it and stood for some time with his face to the opening as the refreshing water sprayed over him.

The cell door creaked open. "You have five minutes, miss," Mark said before locking Rachel inside with Troy.

"Rachel," Troy said in disbelief. He ran his hand back through his wet hair. "What are you doing here? You were supposed to take the stage."

"I know. I know. But the thought struck me that if I returned home early, Papa would wonder why. And then I saw Rod and heard you'd been—arrested. I couldn't leave you!"

"Does your father know about the arrest?"

Rachel shook her head sadly. "Rod made sure to send him a wire. He has several witnesses coming as soon as the stage line can get them here.

"Oh, Troy, hold me."

"I'm a little soggy." He grinned.

"I don't care. Troy, I'm so scared!"

"That makes two of us," he quipped as he put his arms around her trembling form. "I—I wish you didn't have to live through this again."

"Oh, Troy, I love you so much! I don't understand why God is allowing this to happen to you—to us." She hugged him tightly, wishing she'd never have to let go, then pulled back suddenly. "Troy, do you have a lawyer?"

"You know I can't afford a lawyer."

"My father could afford to get you one, but I doubt he would."

"Your father will probably be glad if I hang. It would solve the problem of us being together."

"Troy, please don't say that. Papa would never wish you ill. He just—"

"He just wants a son-in-law with an upstanding family background and a tidy bankroll. Neither of which describes me."

Rachel turned and walked a few steps away from him. "It's not like you to be like this, Troy."

"Like what?"

"Bitter."

Troy sat dejected on the edge of the bed and put his head in his hands. "How am I supposed to be?" he moaned. "I've lived in the shadow of my outlaw father all these years, somehow managing to eke out a living for Mama and Angie, blessed with almost marrying you. Then this! Accused of murder! Nearly lynched! Facing a second trial! I asked the Lord last night to encourage me, and He did. But now—now I feel all tight inside. I'm confused. I feel like God's abandoned me, and that ..." He paused and looked up at her, his eyes betraying his emotional anguish. "you will, too."

Rachel sat beside him, took his right hand, squeezed it gently, then leaned her head against his broad shoulder. "Yesterday, when I said nothing would stop me from loving you, I meant it. Nothing and no one will keep me from marrying you, Troy Daniels."

"A nice sentiment, Rachel, but all it would take to be destroyed is one word from your father or a rope."

Rachel sat with Troy, tears streaming down her face, until Sheriff Kirby announced her time was up. She knew what Troy said was true. It was out of her hands. But she was determined to keep praying for God to give her the desire of her heart, even though it looked impossible.

As she stood up to leave, she squeezed Troy's hand again. "Let's be strong—for each other." She bent over and kissed his forehead, then followed the sheriff to his office.

CHAPTER 12

Biding Time

Tess was worried about Mary. She and Angie hadn't been to visit or come for the meals they were used to eating together. Instead, Mary had purchased meals for themselves and Troy from the small café in town. Deciding to do something to encourage them, Tess knocked on the door of their room.

Mary slowly opened it and peered out. Her eyes were swollen from crying. She looked tired and haggard from sleepless nights spent primarily in prayer.

"Mary," Tess said compassionately, "I've missed yer company. I'd like ya both to join Pop and me tonight fer supper."

"That's very kind of you, Mom, but … I don't know as we'd be very good company. Besides, you might not want to be associated with us anymore. Not after what's happened."

"Nonsense, that makes it all the more necessary. Ya can't let yerself believe fer one minute that we would think that fine boy of yers could be guilty of … well, it jest can't be true, and that's a fact. Pop's plannin' on testifyin' on his behalf."

Mary's face brightened. "He is? He'd do that for Troy?" Her eyes filled with tears as Tess reached out her arms and took her friend into a comforting embrace. Mary thought there couldn't be any more tears left inside her, but they released themselves in yet another torrent. "You don't know how much that means to me."

"Well, ya jest come on upstairs in about a half an hour. Everythin' will be ready."

"Would you like some help?" Mary offered, gently pulling back and wiping her eyes.

"Ya have enough goin' on without needin' to help in the kitchen. We'd jest be delighted to have ya eat with us again. It's gotten to be mighty lonesome without yer company."

"You've been so good to us, Mom. I don't know what we would have done without you and Pop."

"Well, it's like ya told me—the Lord takes care of His own. And, I got me a feelin' He'll be takin' care of Troy, too."

"You're right," Mary agreed. "Here I've been tellin' you about the Lord, and my faith seems mighty weak right now."

"Well, ya jest freshen up a mite, then come join us fer supper. Some of my cookin' will liven ya up. I'm not meanin' to brag, but it's a heap better than the food at the café."

Mary laughed. "That's the truth, for sure!"

"Smells wonderful!" Mary said when they entered the little upstairs apartment.

"Oh, I'm so glad to hear ya say that," Tess remarked. "I enjoy cookin' fer others, especially when they's some of my favorite people. Now, jest set yerselves down. I made some of them biscuits ya like so much, Angie, dear."

"Thank you, Mom! I've been thinking about your biscuits!" Angie was thrilled to be spending time with Mom and Pop again. She'd never known her grandparents, so the elderly couple filled a void in her young life.

"Well," chimed in Jeremy, "ya should have jest come upstairs and asked fer some. Ya know, the both of ya are like family."

"Troy, too?" Angie asked hesitantly.

70

Jeremy cleared his throat, choking back the emotion.

"Yes, sweetheart," Tess said, coming to her husband's assistance. "Troy, too. Someday soon, he'll be back around the table with us. Ya jest wait and see. Yer Mama has more faith than she realizes. She's been prayin' fer that brother of yers. I'm sure ya have, too, haven't ya?"

"I pray all the time. I know Troy couldn't do that awful thing people are sayin' he did. He's a wonderful brother. He's never mean to anyone."

"Course not." Tess sat down between Jeremy and Angie and held out her hands to both.

"What are ya doin', woman?" Pop asked.

"I'm gettin' ready fer the blessin'. I've missed it."

Jeremy gave her a sideways glance. He liked Mary and her children, but what he'd been afraid of seemed to be happening. Their religion was rubbing off on Tess.

"Mary, would ya do the honors?" Tess asked before Jeremy could say anything to the contrary."

"I'd love to." Mary, Angie, and Tess bowed their heads as Jeremy stared at them. "Lord, we can't thank you enough for these dear friends. They offered us shelter and food when we had nowhere to go and no provisions left. They're willing to stand by us now in our darkest hour. Please, bless them, Lord—"

"And, Lord, bless Troy and bring him back to his family real soon!" Tess interjected, surprising herself and everyone else.

"Amen!" Angie shouted.

Pop cleared his throat again as Tess started dishing out the beef stew.

CHAPTER 13

Visitors

"You've got visitors, boy."

Troy was expecting it to be his mother, Rachel, Mom, or Pop, who had faithfully visited him daily for the past three weeks. But when the sheriff unlocked the cell, Rod and Toby entered. Troy felt sick to his stomach. He turned away from them.

"I'll give you five minutes with him, no more," Mark told Rod.

"Five minutes is all we need, Sheriff," Rod assured him.

An awkward silence ensued. Troy didn't want Rod to know just how nervous he was, so he acted as if they weren't in the room, pretending to be calm, even though his heart was racing and pounding in his ears.

"Just thought you'd like to know the circuit judge is in town," Rod announced. "Apparently, he's known around these parts as 'the hanging judge.'"

So that's why Rod's here—to intimidate me. "It's—it's nice of you to tell me, Rod."

"The trial's set for the end of the week, boy," Toby added in a superior tone of voice. "I'm gonna be a witness!"

Troy couldn't help himself. He spun around abruptly and faced him. "Well now, that's a comforting thought, Mr. Jenson," he said sarcastically, then questioned Rod. "How can you use him as a witness when he wasn't even there?"

Toby answered for Rod. "I'm a witness to how you tried to hide who you were like you was guilty of somethin'. How I tried to pry some answers from you—"

"I told you who I was. I just didn't let on who my pa was because, frankly, it was no one else's business," he added with a jab at Toby's hobby as a busybody. "Besides, I knew his reputation would have pegged me as no good, just like it's pegged me as a murderer!"

"I've got witnesses, Troy," Rod prodded him. "Eye-witnesses. The same ones who were at your trial back home. They came into town on the morning stage."

"You have witnesses to the fact that I jumped out the window of your house and ran off after the shooting, not that I committed any crime."

"Oh, as if breaking into my house in the middle of the night wasn't a crime itself!" Rod sputtered.

"I told you—I was forced to go!"

"Right. Forced to go by your own pa."

"Yes, by my pa and four of his drunken gang!

"Rod, we were best friends when we were little children! I worked for your family for the last several years. You know me! You know I would never do anything to hurt Jessica or anyone else, for that matter!"

"We were friends before everyone discovered how your pa got his money—by robbing banks!

"As far as you working for us—my father was willing to take a chance on you in spite of your unscrupulous reputation. After he passed, Mother felt obligated to keep you on—for your Mama's sake more than yours."

"That was my pa's reputation, not mine!"

"Maybe your pa put you up to it. Maybe you came to our house looking for a job, putting on a front during that time, so you could size up the place and find out where the valuables were kept, so you could come back and lead him to the loot."

"That's exactly why my pa forced me to go. But I didn't lead him to anything. Number one—because I didn't know where your valuables were kept. Number two—I wouldn't have told him if I did!"

"You told him, all right. Then my sister saw you, and you killed her to shut her up!"

Troy shook his head, finding it hard to believe Rod could actually think he was guilty of such a heinous crime. "No! No! Besides, I told every detail of what happened that night during the trial back home. You *know* I'm innocent!"

"Do I? I've got new evidence, and it all points right to you, Troy!"

Troy was exasperated. "What new evidence?"

"You lied in your testimony. You lied to save your worthless neck!"

"No. No!"

"You got any witnesses, boy?" Toby taunted him.

Troy sank onto the edge of the bed and looked away from them again, struggling to control his emotions.

"Course he does," Rod mocked. "He's got his pa! Maybe you ought to send for him, Troy. He'd let everyone know how things really were, now, wouldn't he?"

"That could be real excitin'!" Toby chimed in. "Maybe they'd hang him alongside you, boy!" He pulled up tightly on Troy's shirt collar to simulate a hanging, then quickly released it.

Troy straightened his shirt and looked Rod squarely in the eyes. "I do have one witness you've forgotten about, Rod."

"Oh really? Like who?"

"God," Troy said softly.

Rod and Toby snickered.

"Times up, gentlemen," Mark announced as he unlocked the cell door.

Rod turned back to Troy just before leaving. "Unfortunately for you, God won't be there to give His testimony of what happened."

"Don't underestimate Him," Troy responded.

Rod laughed again. "Pleasant dreams, Troy."

"Pleasant dreams. Pleasant dreams." Rod's words echoed in Troy's head as he tried to fall asleep that night. The bed was uncomfortable at best. The air was hot and still, suffocating, without so much as the slightest breeze coming through the tiny, barred window.

But it was the memories. Again. Memories of the night Rod tried to take the law into his own hands. Memories of the night he was nearly lynched. He tossed and turned until the recollections magnified, morphing into a nightmare.

He could see himself pacing anxiously back and forth across the front room of the tiny cabin his family called home. His breathing was heavy, his thoughts wild and frantic.

"Troy," his mother pleaded with him from the platform rocker where she sat nervously knitting a blanket, her needles clicking rapidly but accomplishing little. "Sit down. It's over. That horrible ordeal with your father and his gang is over. The trial is over. You weren't found to be guilty."

"I wasn't declared to be innocent either." His brown eyes flashed with a terrifying fire that seemed to flicker like a lantern in the dimly lit room. "It's not over, Mama! It's just the beginning."

Then, through the window, he saw torches lighting up the night sky as if it were daylight. Holding each torch was a man, woman, or child. It seemed as though every person in the entire town of Tucson was surrounding the house and shouting, "Murderer! Hang him! Hang him!"

Rod appeared in the window, reaching his hand through, trying to grasp Troy. The door flew open. A noose dangled down from the middle of the doorjamb.

"No! No!" Troy shouted, sitting up suddenly, his hand protectively covering his throat. He was drenched in sweat, gasping for breath. Darkness surrounded him. He reached out and felt the hard cement wall; he was in jail in Spring River, not their home in Tucson. Eventually, his breathing calmed. He closed his eyes. "It was just a dream," he reassured himself. "Just a dream—for now."

CHAPTER 14

The Unexpected

The next day at noon, Jeremy came to see Troy.

"I can only give you five minutes with him, Pop," Mark told him. "And I'm sorry, but I've got to check that bowl you've got there."

"Check the ..." Jeremy fussed. "Ya think I got some file hidden in there, do ya? Or maybe Mom baked it in this here piece of pie!" He held the plate up for the sheriff to see. "Better check that, too, Sheriff!"

"I'm sorry, Pop. It's just regulations."

"Regalations! Hmph!" Jeremy snorted. "Yer just jealous cause she didn't make ya nothin'."

Mark laughed. "Well, now, I wouldn't mind if you brought me some of her good cookin' from time to time. Course, you're such a selfish old coot," he teased.

"Selfish! Who are ya callin' selfish? Old coot!"

"Simmer down, Pop. Remember, you've only got five minutes."

Troy glanced up at his former employer as he entered the cell.

"I brung ya some stew. Mom sent it."

"Tell her I'm grateful, sir, but I ain't hungry."

"Ya got to keep up yer strength, boy."

79

"For what? So they can hang me?" Troy sighed and sat down on the bed. "I'm—I'm sorry, sir."

Jeremy sat beside him. "It's all right, son. I can't imagine how this must be fer ya."

"I know I'll be in Heaven, Pop. It's not death itself that's botherin' me. Death for the Christian is like—going home. But the humiliation of being hanged—being in front of all those people, feeling the rope around … I've experienced it over and over again in my mind."

He got up and walked over to the barred window. "It's not just me I'm thinking about. It's Mama, Angie, Rachel, you, and Mom—all the people I've met since we came to this town. It's everyone …" He paused, finding it difficult to say the words. "It's everyone thinking I'm a murderer."

"I don't think that, Troy. I ain't known ya fer long, but I'm a right good judge of character." He looked over at the little Bible sitting on the crate. "I don't rightly see how ya could believe in that there book like ya says ya do and be guilty of what that Rod fellow is sayin'."

"I do believe in that Book, Pop. I believe everything it says. If I didn't have God on my side, I think I'd die right here and now."

Troy had been praying for an opportunity to speak with Pop about his soul. He saw the old man's words as an opportunity. "That's another thing I've been bothered about, Pop. I know you asked me not to talk to you about it, but—"

"Hold on, son. I didn't bring it up so ya'd be preachin' at me. Jest wanted ya to know I think yer innocent."

"Please, Pop," Troy pleaded earnestly, turning away from the window. "I may be dead in a few days! I may not have another chance to talk with you about accepting Christ as your Savior."

"Like I told ya afore, there ain't no need of me gittin' religion. Me and Mom are happy jest the way we is."

"It's not a religion, Pop. It's a relationship with Jesus Christ. It's asking Him to come into your heart and forgive you of your sin."

"I ain't as bad as some folks, Troy. I ain't like your pa ..." As soon as he blurted out the words, Jeremy realized how deeply hurtful they were. "I'm—I'm sorry, boy. I shouldn't have said that."

Troy stared blankly at the floor. "I understand, sir. I know you're nothing like my pa, but in God's eyes, sin is sin. The Bible says, 'For all have sinned and come short of the glory of God.'"

"I'm a good-livin' person. I reckon my good works will outweigh my bad ones when I go to meet my Maker."

"But that's not how it works, Pop. We don't get to Heaven by our good works. We get there because Jesus paid the price—"

"That'd be enough," Jeremy said adamantly. "I don't want to hear no more."

Troy was disappointed. He sighed and resigned himself to the old man's wishes. "Yes, sir."

"Times just about up, Pop," Mark called from the other room.

Jeremy put his hand on Troy's shoulder. His voice was soft, comforting. "I'll be back later, Troy. Ya try and eat somethin', all right?"

Troy nodded in agreement.

"And don't ya go gettin' lazy on me while yer here in this pigpen." He raised his voice louder for Mark's benefit. "I say, this here jail looks like a pigpen!"

"I hear ya, Pop!" came the spirited reply.

Pop winked at Troy. "Yer gonna have lots of catchin' up to do back at the shop when this whole thing is over."

"I hope so, sir," Troy replied.

Angie came running into the sheriff's office. "Sheriff! Sheriff! I got to find Pop! Mama said he came to see Troy."

"He's right in there," Mark answered, retrieving the keys from his desk and unlocking the wooden door that led to the cells.

"Angie!" Troy wished she hadn't seen him locked in a metal cage. "What are you doing here?"

Seeing her big brother behind the thick steel bars made Angie feel like crying. But, knowing she had an important message, she bit her lower lip, scrunched her eyes to keep back the tears, and tried to be brave. "Pop, Mama says you're to come quickly!"

Pop was surprised at the usually quiet girl's agitation. "What are ya hollerin' about?"

"It's Mom. Mama says something's happened to her, something about her heart. She said I was to fetch you quick like."

"Somethin's happened to Mom?"

Mark unlocked the cell door and let Jeremy out. The old man was shaking as he grasped Angie's hand, hobbled out of the office, and walked as quickly as his unsteady legs would take him down the street to the mercantile.

Mark started to lock the cell door.

"Sheriff, I've probably got no right to ask this," Troy said. "I'll understand if you say, 'No,' but—please, will you let me go see Mom?"

Mark crossed his arms, then put one hand on his chin and rubbed it slightly, as was his custom when deep in thought. "I'm not sure folks would take too kindly to that, Troy." He rubbed his chin some more, then sighed. "It's against my better judgment, but ... I'll have to take some precautions and go with you so no one can say you were trying to escape. Otherwise, that Rod fellow is liable to shoot you!"

"I understand, sir."

Mark put Troy in handcuffs, took his gun out of its holster, and cautiously opened the door. "All right. Let's go," he said, motioning for Troy to walk in front of him.

When Jeremy and Angie arrived at the upstairs living quarters, Mom was seated in the rocking chair with Mary beside her. Mary placed Tess's cold, worn hand in Jeremy's. Then, she walked silently to Angie, putting her arm around the tearful little girl.

"Is she gonna die, Mama?" Angie whispered.

"Shh—it's all right, Angie. God cares about Mom. Nothing can happen apart from Him. We have to trust that He knows best." Her last words were more for her own comfort than Angie's as she thought of her beloved son sitting in a jail cell awaiting a possible hanging. A chill passed through her; she shuddered.

"Tess," Jeremy said, holding her hand with his left and stroking her hair with his right. "What happened?"

Tess smiled weakly at the man she had loved for over fifty years. Her breathing was labored as she struggled to talk. "I was hopin' ya'd git here before—"

"Afore what? What's wrong?"

"I'm goin' home."

"Home? What do ya mean? This is our home."

Tess shook her head. "I'm goin' to be with Jesus."

Jeremy glanced at Mary. He was concerned, confused, and wondering if his wife had lost her senses. "Why ain't the doc been sent fer?"

I—" Mary started to answer.

"Don't be cross with her, Jeremy," Tess said. "I told her not to bother. Ain't no use in troublin' him."

"Troublin' him! That's what he's there fer, ain't it? I'm goin' to git him—"

"No, please, stay here with me. I want ya with me."

"Don't try to talk none. Save yer strength." Jeremy urged, then instructed Mary, "I don't care what she told ya. Go git the doc. Ya know where his office is?"

"Yes, I—"

"Doc's out of town deliverin' Mrs. Anderson's baby," Mark said as he and Troy entered the room.

Angie threw her arms around her big brother. "Oh, Troy, you're home!"

"Only for a little while, Sis."

Angie noticed the cuffs on Troy's hands and eyed the sheriff suspiciously. "He's not gonna hurt you, is he?"

"No. No, honey, he's not going to hurt me. The sheriff brought me here so I could see Mom."

"I'll wait for you at the bottom of the stairs, Troy," Mark said, wanting to give Troy and his family a little time together.

Mom's face brightened. "Troy, I'm so glad ya came. Don't ya give up on Pop, Troy. Ya tell him—tell him about Jesus like yer sweet Mama told me."

Troy looked at his mother for an explanation while Jeremy shifted his feet self-consciously.

"Mom and I were talking about how to get saved," Mary explained, "how to know for sure she was going to Heaven."

"I had jest confessed my sins to Jesus and asked Him to come into my heart and be my Savior when ..." Tess grimaced as another sharp pain shot through her heart.

"Troy!" Jeremy said in an agitated voice. "Tell the sheriff to go git the doc! I don't care where he is or what he's doin'. He's got to come! Well, go on, boy!"

"Yes, sir," Troy answered, giving his mother a furtive look. The Anderson's ranch was five miles out of town. They both knew the doctor would never get there in time. He turned to leave.

"Troy. Troy, come closer, dear." Mom's breathing was coming in spurts. She rested her cheek on her husband's hand and looked up at him, her eyes pleading. "Jeremy, please ... let Troy talk to ya about Jesus. I want ... to see ya again."

"Stop talkin' foolishness. Ya ain't goin' nowhere. Yer gonna be jest fine."

Then to Troy, he shouted, "I done told ya to go tell the sheriff to fetch the doc!"

"Yes, sir."

Tess cried out in pain. Her face was ashen white; it was evident she didn't have long. She grasped ahold of the corner of Troy's shirt. Her voice was barely audible. "Please, Troy, don't ya ... give up on Pop. He's a might ... stubborn. Don't ya quit ... talkin' to him about ..."

84

Suddenly, she sat up straight, her face a portrait of glowing peace. "They's comin' fer me!" she said excitedly.

Thinking she was delirious, Jeremy felt his wife's forehead. It was cool, clammy. He turned toward Troy with an angry countenance. "That doc needs to be comin'!"

Troy sighed, backed away, and told himself not to take Pop's anger personally; he knew the words were the result of extreme grief. He also realized nothing could be done to change the inevitable.

"It's angels, Jeremy! I can see them. I ..." Another spasm ripped through Mom's chest as she slumped forward.

Jeremy bent over his beloved helpmeet and held her close. "Tess! Tessie!" Her body went limp; she was gone.

CHAPTER 15

The Funeral

The trial was delayed a few days due to Tess William's funeral. Troy, though shackled, was permitted to attend. He and the sheriff followed at the back of the processional as it wended its way to the gravesite. There, they stood beside Mary and Angie.

Mom had been a popular fixture in Spring River. Tess Johnson had been born in a little farmhouse about two miles from town before the town existed. She watched it grow around her during her childhood, met and married Jeremy Williams in the summer of 1840, then spent the rest of her days at the mercantile cheerily serving the people she loved. The men respected her; the ladies admired her. The children adored the sweet, nurturing woman who always made sure they didn't leave the store until she gave them a piece of penny candy.

Though the entire town had come to express their sympathy, Jeremy, in a state of listless shock, was unresponsive to the words of comfort and encouragement offered to him. Troy was saddened to see the once robust, cheerful man physically supported and led about by two of the town's men. He longed to fulfill his promise to Mom to talk with Pop about the Savior, but it was useless—his words would only fall on deaf ears.

There was no preacher in Spring River—hadn't been for several years, so Mayor Jackson led the service.

Troy fidgeted through the long oration. He felt conspicuous and vulnerable. Hearing whispers and sensing that people were staring at him occasionally, he looked up only one time—at Rachel. Once their eyes met, they held onto the longing gaze until Rachel's father broke the transitory spell with a steely glower that caused Troy to look away self-consciously, then down at his feet.

Finally, the last shovel of sod was thrown over the casket. Mary lovingly placed the daises she and Angie had gathered that morning on the mound of earth covering her friend's cold body. *She's not really down there.* The comforting truth brought peace to Mary's troubled mind. *She's walking on streets of gold. I just wish I could have given her the afghan. She'll never know it was for her. Perhaps, if we're still here by Christmas, I can give it to Pop.* She gasped as she wondered if Troy would be with them at Christmas.

"I'm sorry, ma'am," Sheriff Kirby whispered to Mary. "I need to get Troy back to the jail before an onslaught of busybodies or revenge seekers swarm around him.

Mary nodded and looked up at her son. "I'll come tonight with your dinner, Troy."

"Thanks, Mama," he said as he and the sheriff left. Troy was glad to be returning to the cell; his shoulders were beginning to ache from the awkward position of his hands, and the cuffs were chafing his wrists.

Troy and Mark walked quickly away from the group of mourners, although not fast enough to avoid Toby's shuffling feet and irritating voice. The man was huffing and puffing, trying to keep up with them, but he was bound and determined to take every advantage before the trial to be seen near Troy. Being close to an official criminal gave him a sense of notoriety and added an exciting adventure to his otherwise dreary days of measuring, cutting, and stitching fabric.

"Mind if I join you *fine* people," Toby sneered.

Mark, determined that his prisoner would not suffer unnecessarily, allowed Troy to decide.

"It's all right, Sheriff. He'll need to get it off his chest sometime. It might as well be now."

Toby, quite pleased with his query's outcome, strutted beside them. "Shame about Mom, ain't it?" he remarked casually, trying to start up a conversation.

His two companions muttered in assent and continued walking. Not to be ignored, Toby spoke up again. "Guess that don't leave you with many witnesses, does it, boy?"

"No, sir," Troy said flatly, "I guess it doesn't."

"I mean, with Mom gone and Pop ... well, he certainly ain't in no condition to attest to your character, let alone your innocence."

Though irritated by the verbal abuse, Troy was determined to hide his emotions. However, Mark was becoming increasingly agitated with the troublesome nuisance.

"By the way," Toby continued, "I met Rachel's father. Fine man. Fine man." He glanced slyly at Troy and was delighted to see the color rise in the boy's face. "Heard he's forbidden her to testify. Looks like you ain't got much of a chance."

Mark exploded. "You're not going to have much of a chance if you don't make yourself scarce!"

"Just a minute, Sheriff," Toby said with self-righteous indignation. "You've got no right to intimidate me!"

"And you have no right to intimidate my prisoner!" Mark retorted.

"Well!" huffed Toby. "You have a lot of nerve! You may not realize to whom you're speakin'. I'm a valuable witness in this case."

"I realize it, all right," came the reply, "and I hope you realize to whom *you* are speaking! If you don't leave this young man alone, I might have to lock you up for disobeying an officer of the law!"

Troy was relieved, humored, and horrified by the sheriff's words. He couldn't imagine—he didn't want to imagine—being locked up with Toby!

"You'll hear about this at the next town meetin'!" Toby protested. "I'll tell them you give the criminal more rights than the victim!"

"The only one you're a victim of is yourself!" Mark said, shocked at his own candor.

"Well!" Toby arched his unruly eyebrows and stalked off in disgust. He continued muttering about dishonest sheriffs and miserable creatures until disappearing into his shop.

"That man reminds me of a weasel!" Mark confided to Troy.

CHAPTER 16

Rod's New Evidence

Monday of the following week began with clouds that grew darker and darker as the day progressed. Now, droplets of rain were pattering on the rooftops. Mary looked at the ominous sky and wondered if she'd return home in time to avoid the inevitable cloudburst.

"I brought some supper for Troy," she called from outside the sheriff's office. I wondered if you'd be so kind as to open the door for me."

"Of course. Of course," Mark stated, coming to her aid as quickly as possible. "Here, let me take that for you." He carefully lifted the platter of food and placed it on his desk, then retrieved his keys.

Mary picked up the platter and followed him through the door that led to the hallway and two cells.

"You've got company, Troy."

Troy glanced up from the bed where he'd been lying. "Nice to see a friendly face." He forced a smile as Mark unlocked the cell door and his mother entered.

"Take all the time you need, ma'am," Mark told her. "Just let me know when you're ready to go." He locked the door behind her.

Mary was genuinely grateful for the sheriff's kindness. He had been very accommodating of the daily time she spent with Troy. "Thank you, sheriff."

Troy stood. "Here, Mama, sit down," he said as he took the platter and set it on the wooden crate. Mary placed her shawl beside her as Troy removed the cloth covering from the food. "Fried chicken! You're spoiling me," he teased.

Mary smiled at him, then burst into tears.

"Mama, what is it? What's wrong?"

Mary looked around the dismal surroundings and wondered how her son could ask such a question. *Is there a level lower than hopeless?* she wondered. She dreaded telling Troy the news she'd heard but knew it was necessary.

"Rachel's all right, isn't she? I mean, I saw her from a distance at the funeral, but she hasn't been to see me since then."

Mary nodded her head in the affirmative.

"And Angie?"

"Angie's fine."

"Pop. How's he doing?"

Mary sighed. "Pop just sits in his little parlor, staring out the window."

"Does he eat anything?"

"A little. Not enough, though. He's thin, to begin with. He can't stand to lose much weight. Angie and I took over the store for him today." She forced a smile, then began rubbing her hands together nervously.

"What is it, Mama? There's something you're not telling me."

"The trial's been rescheduled for tomorrow, Troy."

"I figured as much."

"Mom's funeral delayed it long enough so the expensive lawyer Rod sent for could arrive. They say he's the best in these parts."

Troy turned away from her, head down, and didn't answer.

"Troy, you don't have a lawyer! You don't even have any witnesses!"

He turned and faced her. "I can defend myself, Mama. Besides, I've got character witnesses. I know Pop ain't up to testifying, but I've got you." He paused, then added, "And Rachel."

"I'm your mother, Troy. Everyone will expect me to stand up for you. And Rachel's your fiancée. But ..." Unable to look at him, she gazed at the ceiling and drummed her fingers on the wooden ridge of the bed. "Rachel's father ..."

Troy crossed over to her, knelt on one knee to be eye-level, and took her hands in his. "What about him, Mama?"

Tears escaped as Mary struggled to hold back the full force of her emotions.

"Mama?"

This time, Mary looked directly into the depths of Troy's brown eyes. "He won't let Rachel testify on your behalf. He won't even let her come see you. That's why she hasn't been here since the funeral. He doesn't want her to have anything to do with you!"

"So it *is* true." Troy mentally struggled with the thought of losing Rachel but didn't let on to Mary except to say, "I was hoping it was only a rumor, but I should have expected it. If I were Mr. Wagner and I thought my daughter's fiancé was guilty of ... I wouldn't want my daughter associated with a murderer, either."

"How did you know? Who told you?"

"Toby."

"Toby! When did he talk to you?"

"On the way back from the funeral. He followed the sheriff and me through town until he came to his shop."

"Oh, that man! He reminds me of—"

"Of a weasel?"

"Yes!"

"You kind of have to feel sorry for him, though," Troy remarked. "He probably doesn't have any real friends."

"It's his own fault," Mary snapped. "I—I'm sorry, Troy," she apologized immediately. "I shouldn't have said that. It's just that ... when I think of tomorrow and all the terrible things people will say and think about you. I—I don't know if I can bear it."

"Maybe it would be best if you didn't go to the trial, Mama."

"No. No, Troy. I'm not leaving you there by yourself. I don't know what I can do, but ... I'm not deserting you, son."

Troy sat beside her, cocked his head back, and stared at the ceiling.

Mary studied him for a few minutes. He looked so handsome, strong, and young—much like his father when she first met him. Yet, they were so different. Colby was insensitive, callous, and wicked. Troy was thoughtful, gentle, and compassionate.

"Mama," Troy said cautiously, wanting to reveal what was uppermost in his heart yet dreading her reaction. "I have a favor to ask."

"What is it, son?" Mary reached for his hand.

"It's about Pop. I—I promised Mom I'd talk to him, but the way he is now ..."

"He'll probably snap out of it later when Mom's death isn't so fresh in his mind."

"I hope so. I keep wondering about it. He's rejected God's Word. He thinks he's good enough to get to Heaven on his own."

"I guess it's sometimes harder for folks who've lived a moral, upright life to understand that they're sinners in need of a Savior."

"I suppose you're right. I just hope it isn't too late for him." Troy was silent for a few minutes, then broached the subject he'd been leading up to. "Mama, promise me that if I—"

"No, Troy! Don't say it! Please don't say it!"

"I have to face reality, Mama." Tears formed in his eyes. "I know it's hard to talk about, but ... promise me, please promise me that if I ... die ... you'll talk to Pop. Please, Mama!"

She buried her head in her hands and sobbed.

"I'm sorry, Mama. I shouldn't have mentioned it."

Mary looked at him through eyes blurred by tears. That he should be so concerned about someone else when he might be at the threshold of death's door touched a chord of profound admiration in her heart. "No, Troy. Don't be sorry." She wiped the tears from her face. "I promise," she said resolutely. There was more she needed to share, but the words were stuck in her throat.

Troy stood beside her as she got ready to leave, helping her fix the shawl around her shoulders. But rather than call to Mark to unlock the door, she stood quietly, fidgeting with the fringe on her wrap.

Her silence made Troy suspicious. "Is there more, Mama?"

Mary sighed. "I should have told you before, but I couldn't. Rod wanted it to be kept a secret from you, and I didn't have the heart to tell you. But you need to know before the trial." She paused, biting her lip to stifle the frustrated scream inside her that wanted to escape. "His mother's been in town ever since before Mom died. She came to testify against you. She's been telling everyone ... and to think that you and Rod were best friends when you were little!" Unable to continue, she began crying again.

Troy spoke gently to her. "Mama, what is it she's telling people?" He put his hand on her shoulder and said kindly but firmly, "Mama."

"That she saw you shoot Jessica!"

Troy was stunned. "What?" He knew it was impossible; he hadn't been the one who murdered her. Then it became apparent to him. "Rod's new evidence."

"What?"

"Nothing." There was an awkward silence for a few moments. "You don't ... you don't believe her, do you?"

"Of course not! But everyone else will. Oh, Troy, there's no way out of this! They're going to hang you!" she cried. "They're going to hang you!"

Troy swallowed hard, struggling with his own emotions. If there were ever an impossible situation, this was it. Humanly speaking, she was right—there was no way out. He put his arms around her. "Mama, do you remember when we first got here and talked about trusting the Lord?"

Mary nodded. "It's easy to talk about."

"I know. But Mama," he continued earnestly, "I've had lots of time to think, pray, and read God's Word. Even before you came here today, I guessed I'll be found guilty unless God works a miracle." He cleared his dry throat. "I don't know why the Lord would let that happen, why He wouldn't clear my name. But, He gave me a verse just yesterday that I've been clinging to. I've read it so many times before, but—it never had as much meaning as it does now. It's Romans 8:28, 'And we know that all things work together for good to them that love God, to them who are the called according to His purpose.'"

CHAPTER 17

The Trial

T roy stood by the window, grasping the steel bars until his fingers were white. Every nerve in his body tingled; he felt weak and trembly.

Leaving his post, he reached again for his worn Bible. Without it, he knew he couldn't face this day. He turned to the Scripture he had read earlier that morning, *'What time I am afraid, I will trust in thee. In God I will praise His Word, in God I have put my trust; I will not fear what flesh can do unto me.'*

The keys rattled on the other side of the wooden door. "It's time, son," Mark said sympathetically, wishing, at that moment, he had any job but sheriff.

Troy laid the Bible back down on the crate and stood patiently, silently, as his ankles were locked in leg irons and his hands cuffed behind him.

"I'm sorry to have to do this to you, boy," Mark admitted.

Troy tried to respond, but the words stuck in his throat, so he nodded instead.

School had disbanded a week early so the trial could be held in the church. It was the only building in town large enough to house the number of people expected. Troy walked meekly ahead of the sheriff, trying to ignore the whispers all around him as latecomers pushed and shoved their way through the church doors, hoping to get a seat inside.

"Out of the way," Mark ordered as he and Troy were jostled through the crowd into the sanctuary.

Once inside, Troy took a deep breath to steady his nerves. On the way over, he had pondered his strategy and concluded that there was no strategy. He had no witnesses. He no longer had Mom, Pop, or Rachel. The only ones who could prove his innocence were outlaws two territories away. Besides, they wouldn't willingly come into a court of law. His mother could verify that he'd been forced to go against his will that night. But, as she had said, people would expect her to be defensive, so it was doubtful her words would help. Judging from the kindness he'd been shown by Sheriff Kirby and his words of encouragement minutes earlier, Troy was confident the man would put in a good word for him if he could. However, as an officer of the law, everyone would expect him to be impartial. It was true—God was his only witness; all Troy could do was hope in His mercy and pray for a miracle.

Troy kept his head down, noticing every knot in the floorboards as they walked to the front. Being the son of a hated outlaw, he was accustomed to being humiliated. He'd had nothing to be proud of his entire life, nothing that would make him an accepted and respected part of society. But being stared at as if he were the lowest scum on earth—someone who would kill an innocent child–had been the most shameful part of the ordeal. He had lived through it in Tucson; now, he was reliving it in Spring River. He prayed for courage to face the strangers in the audience, the recent acquaintances he'd made, and those he'd known all his life; courage to defend himself; courage to accept the verdict no matter what. *Perhaps it would be easier if I pleaded guilty and let them hang me,* he thought. *At least I could be done with it once and for all. I'd be in Heaven—forever.* He reflected on the verses about the eternal abode of the saved he'd read about in Revelation. They had been a great comfort to him during the last few days.

Mark removed Troy's shackles and motioned for him to sit in the defendant's chair at the front of the room. Troy glanced at the twelve people who would serve as his jury. Since he didn't recognize them, he assumed they were cowhands from the neighboring ranches who didn't frequent the mercantile and wouldn't have a connection to him. His heart sank. Cowboys were a rough-and-tumble lot. *They'd probably be thrilled to see a hanging,* he thought despondently. The odds of him winning the case were slimmer than ever.

Judge Taylor pounded his gavel on the pulpit. "This court is now in session. The defendant, Troy Daniels, will please rise."

Troy rose slowly. His legs were like jelly, his hands clammy, shaking. He clenched and unclenched them into fists to steady them. He still couldn't look at anyone, though he knew his mother was in the front row; in his peripheral vision, he could see the edge of her calico skirt. He could sense her presence and knew she was praying.

"You are accused of murder in the shooting death of one Jessica Marshall. How do you plead?"

It seemed surreal—like a dream, a nightmare from which he'd never awaken. He tried to speak, but his throat felt scratchy and dry. He tried clearing it, but it only felt drier. "I'm not guilty, sir," he finally managed to say.

Immediately, reactions from the crowd filled the hall. The majority were negative, condemning him as a murderer.

Nauseating dizziness overcame Troy. He reached his hand behind him and grasped the back of the chair to keep himself standing, then closed his eyes. *Help me, Lord. Help me!*

"Order!" the judge shouted above the din. "There will be order in this court!"

He looked at Troy. "You may be seated."

Troy sank gratefully onto the chair.

"Mr. James, you may call your first witness."

A tall, distinguished-looking gentleman with gray hair, a full, neatly trimmed beard, and bright blue eyes stood up. "I call Miss Jennifer Woodward to the stand."

The postmaster had been nominated to be the clerk. He took the large Bible from the pulpit and swore in the witness. "Place your left hand on the Bible and raise your right hand. Do you swear to tell the truth, the whole truth, and nothing but the truth, so help you, God?"

Jennifer remembered that night all too well. She trembled at the thought of being so close to a murderer that evening. She'd never known Troy personally, although she'd seen him several times and knew who he was. Everyone in Tucson knew the family of Killer Colby lived in a shack on the outskirts of town. "Yes," she said simply.

"You may be seated."

Mr. James began his questioning. "Miss Woodward, will you tell the court what you saw on the evening of the eighth of January."

"Yes, sir. My sister, Caroline, and I had been visiting a friend down the street from Rod's house. The hour got late, so we decided to head home."

"At approximately what time was that, Miss Woodward?"

"About ten o'clock. There was a full moon, so it was easy to see. Well, anyway, we were passing the Marshall residence when we heard a gunshot. A few moments later, Troy Daniels jumped out of a window and ran down the street. We decided he'd probably robbed them since his family didn't have much money, and his father ..."

She glanced at Troy, who looked up at the same time. Their eyes locked; Jennifer momentarily felt sorry for the young man, who was only a year older than herself. The pained expression on his face at the mention of his father made her hesitate.

"Miss Woodward," the attorney interrupted her reverie. "What did you and your sister do then?"

"What?"

"After you saw Mr. Daniels jump out the window, what did you do?"

"We—we reported him to the sheriff," she replied, her voice quivering.

"That evening or the next day?"

"Immediately, sir. The sheriff arrested him that night."

"I see. You say there was a full moon?"

"Yes, sir."

"There was no mistaking as to whom you saw coming from the Marshall home?"

Troy and Jennifer's gaze met again. Troy wanted to plead with her not to implicate him, yet he knew she spoke the truth. She *had* seen him jump out the window.

Jennifer hesitated, then said confidently, "No, sir. None at all. We were just a few feet from him. He looked right at us before he started running."

"Did the defendant have anything in his hand?"

"Yes, sir. He had a sack."

The courtroom erupted; Judge Taylor called the session back to order.

"Did you see or hear anyone else?" the lawyer continued.

"We heard horses, but we didn't see any."

"Thank you, Miss Woodward." Mr. James turned toward Troy. "Your witness."

His heart racing, Troy rose slowly and walked over to the witness chair as a low undercurrent of voices showed their displeasure with him. His first trial was a blur; he couldn't remember what he or anyone else had said, only that it had ended up in a hung jury. He'd been given a lawyer then, free of charge—appointed through the kindness of Sheriff Wilson. Now, the questioning was up to him. During his incarceration, he'd prayed for wisdom in developing a defense. But, although he had formulated a plan, he knew there wasn't much hope of it swaying a jury in his favor.

"Miss Woodward, would you please tell the court if there is a doorway on the other side of the house from where you saw ..." He paused; the words he needed to say seemed to choke him. "Where you saw the ..." It was difficult not to incriminate himself. "Where you saw *me* jump out the window."

Jennifer was a friend of the Marshalls. She'd been in the house many times and knew the layout well. "Yes. Yes, there is."

"Would that doorway have been in your view at the time?"

"No."

"Then it could have been possible for someone to have left Rod's house on the opposite side of the window without being seen by you or your sister. Is that correct?"

"Yes, I suppose so."

"Is it possible that the horses you heard belonged to others who had been in the home and were riding away from the crime?"

"I guess it's possible."

"Thank you. No further questions, Your Honor."

The judge nodded, Troy sat down, and Mr. James called his next witness. "I call Mr. Toby Jenson to the witness stand."

Troy shifted nervously in his chair as Toby came up from the front row, nestled himself into the witness chair, then sat up very straight and grinned foolishly at the judge. He was delightfully proud to be the only townsperson called as a witness. Yet, despite his cockiness, the whispered word "busybody" echoed around the church auditorium. Troy hoped the man's reputation would destroy his testimony.

"Do you swear to tell the truth, the whole truth, and nothing but the truth, so help you, God?" the clerk uttered.

"I certainly do!" Toby affirmed emphatically, casting a condescending look in Troy's direction.

Troy looked away. The man really did remind one of a weasel.

"Mr. Jenson. I understand you're from this town?"

"Yes, sir. Lived here all my life. I'm a tailor by trade."

"He's a nuisance!" Emma Tucker piped up. Laughter filled the courtroom as Toby glared at her.

"Order! Order!" the judge cried before giving Emma a solemn warning. "There will be no more outbursts from the audience." Then to Mr. James, he added, "Continue."

"Do you know the defendant?"

"I know him," Toby sputtered as if repulsed by the thought.

"Will you please tell the court how you met Mr. Daniels and what transpired in your conversations with him?"

"Be happy to. I come to Pop's store one day, and here was this young fellow. Never saw him before in my life. Well, naturally, I was curious."

"Naturally," Emma muttered under her breath. The judge scowled at her.

Toby cleared his throat and ignored her comment. "I began askin' him questions like who he was, where he was from, how old he was—things like that."

"And what was the defendant's response?"

"He was real—evasive is the word you could say. He wouldn't look me in the eye. He hesitated for a time before tellin' me his last name—like he was *hidin'* somethin'. Well, I got suspicious. I warned Pop, Your Honor. I figured his new help was runnin' from the law. It weren't long before I found out I was right. This Rod fellow come and told us the reason he," Toby nodded his head in Troy's direction, "didn't want none of us to know much about him. It was because he's a murderer!"

The crowd reacted in an uproar. Even though Troy knew a few people in the auditorium believed in his innocence, their comments were drowned out by those calling for his death. Troy glanced over at his mother. She was crying. The sheriff was holding her hand.

"Looks like I was proved right!" Toby added.

"Nothing has been proven yet," the judge replied, irritated with the meddlesome man.

"I understand," Mr. James continued with his questioning, "that you saw the defendant, about a week after his arrival, talking with a young woman."

"Yes, sir. The girl sittin' right over there." He nodded toward Rachel, who momentarily lowered her gaze to the floor.

Mr. Wagner put his arm protectively around his daughter, narrowing his eyes as he glared back at everyone staring at them.

It was the first time during the proceedings that Troy turned around and saw her. As if sensing that Troy was looking at her, Rachel looked up, her bloodshot, swollen eyes conveying the love, empathy, and despair she felt for him.

"He met her at the stage, 'accidental like,'" Toby continued as Troy refocused his attention on his accuser. "I saw them whisperin'. They was lookin' around to make sure no one noticed. Then they met outside later that night, right here in back of the church. It was obvious they was in love. They didn't kiss, mind you. Well, he did kiss her hand. But there *was* huggin' goin' on." There was a ripple of laughter throughout the room. "I questioned him about her the next mornin', and he was real slippery-like about it. Wouldn't give me no direct answer. Turns out she's his fiancée."

Mr. Wagner stood up abruptly. "Not anymore, she's not!" he shouted.

There was another ripple of conversation until the judge brought his gavel down. "Order! Order! There will be no more outbursts from spectators, or they will be asked to leave!

"Continue, Mr. Jenson."

"It wouldn't surprise me if she was an accomplice," he added, gloating at Troy.

"Outrageous!" Mr. Wagner yelled angrily, springing again to his feet.

"Mr. Jenson," the judge stated gravely to Toby, "your insinuation is totally out of line." Then, to the clerk, he added, "Strike Mr. Jenson's last comment from the record."

To Rachel's father, he said firmly but kindly, "Please sit down, sir. I understand how offensive the comment is, so I will not ask you to leave—this time."

"Your witness," Mr. James said to Troy.

Troy shakily rose from his seat and stood in front of Toby. He also wanted to defend Rachel but knew he needed to keep calm, even though the anger he felt inside seemed as though it would boil over and consume him. "Mr. Jenson, isn't it true that I told you my last name the first day we met?"

"Well, yes, but you was hesitant—like you was scared or embarrassed to say it."

"Isn't it also true that I later stated why I hadn't wanted people to know my identity—that I knew my father's reputation would have kept me from getting a job?"

"Well, yes, but—"

"Isn't it also true that you know nothing about me except what others have told you?"

"Well—yes."

"What it amounts to is that you are basing your opinion on speculation and hearsay. You were not a witness to anything but are simply a gossip who likes to be involved in everyone else's business, who thinks he has all the facts, but, in reality, has none!"

"Well, I—" Toby stood and waved his fist in Troy's face. "Now look here, boy, I ain't on trial. *You* are!"

Troy instinctively backed away from him.

"I object!" Mr. James cried as he rose from his seat beside Rod. "The defendant has no right to intimidate my witness."

"Objection overruled," the judge decreed. "Mr. Daniels has every right to question the validity of anyone as a legitimate witness."

"No further questions, Your Honor," Troy said, then sat down, feeling somewhat satisfied that, at least, he had accomplished something in diminishing the man's testimony.

Toby was livid. He stomped out of the courtroom, muttering to himself as murmurs of "busybody" were repeated throughout the room. "This trial's a joke! Out of my way!" he shouted at those crowded in the doorway. "Move!"

The judge waited for Toby to exit, then nodded to Mr. James to proceed. Mr. James called Rod to the witness stand.

"Do you swear to tell the truth, the whole truth, and nothing but the truth, so help you, God?" the clerk repeated.

"Yes, sir."

"Mr. Marshall, please tell the court what happened at your home on January eighth of this year."

Rod scowled at Troy before beginning. "Yes, sir. It was about ten o'clock. Everyone in the house was asleep. I was awakened by a gunshot. At first, I wasn't sure where it had come from. Then, I realized it had been downstairs in the parlor. I heard my mother scream. I rushed down the stairs, and ..." Rod stopped abruptly at the terrifying memory.

"I know this is difficult for you, Mr. Marshall, but please tell us what you saw."

Rod struggled to hold back tears. His mother started sobbing. "It was my little sister, sir. She'd been shot. My mother was down on her knees beside her, rocking Jessica in her arms."

"Your sister was—dead, Mr. Marshall?"

Rod glowered at Troy once more. "Yes, sir," he said sadly.

"Can you explain why the defendant would want to kill your sister?"

"Yes, sir. My family is well-off. When we were younger, Troy's family had money, too—lots of it. Troy's pa told everyone he'd inherited his money. Then a marshal came to town and said he had proof that Colby Daniels had robbed a bank years earlier—before he'd met Troy's ma. That had been his 'inheritance.' Anyway, Troy's pa managed to escape, then started his long career of thievery and murder. Troy and his ma lost just about everything they had trying to pay off debts. From that time on, Troy was jealous of me."

Troy looked over at Rod and shook his head in disbelief. It seemed impossible this was all happening—for the second time.

"It's obvious he's following in his father's footsteps," Rob continued. "He came to rob us that night. My little sister woke up and found him stealing things from the parlor. He didn't want any witnesses, so—"

Troy jumped up from his seat in desperation. "That's not true! Your Honor, it's not true!"

"The defendant will remain silent," the judge ordered. "You will have your chance to defend yourself. Now sit down."

"But, sir—"

"Sit down," the judge repeated firmly. Troy slowly lowered himself onto his chair.

Mr. James questioned Rod further. "You say he came to rob you? Do you have proof of that?"

"Yes, sir. The sheriff found a burlap sack later that night, the one to which Miss Woodward referred. It was filled with money and a few things belonging to my family."

"Please tell the court where the sack was found."

"In some bushes behind Troy's house."

Mr. James nodded to Troy. "Your witness."

It was difficult for Troy to face Rod. At first, his legs seemed leaden, like they couldn't move. When he finally managed to walk the few yards and stand before Rod, his former friend refused to look at him. "Will you please tell the court how long we've known each other?"

"Too long," Rod muttered under his breath.

"Speak up, son," the judge directed. "What did you say?"

"I said I've known him too long."

Mr. James rose from his seat. "Objection, your honor. The question is irrelevant."

"It is not irrelevant," Troy refuted. "You asked Toby Jenson—"

The judge brought his gavel down against the pulpit with a bang. "That will be enough from both of you. Mr. James, since we do not yet know where the defendant is leading with this question, it is too early to determine its relevance. And I will be the one to decide that."

Mr. James acquiesced and sat down. "Yes, Your Honor."

"Proceed," the judge said to Troy.

"Thank you, sir," Troy responded, then asked the question again. "Rod, how long have you and I known each other?"

"Since we were little," Rod answered dully.

"Have you ever known me to be a violent person?"

"No."

"Have you ever known me to carry a gun?"

Rod squirmed uncomfortably; Troy was making points with the jury. Anger welled up inside him. He was more determined than ever to make Troy pay for his crimes. "No."

"Have you ever known me to steal before?"

"No, but I never heard of you breaking into someone's house until that night, either. Deny that!"

"You are out of order, Mr. Marshall," the judge declared before directing the clerk to strike the last remark from the record. "Continue, Mr. Daniels."

Troy was visibly shaken. He was too stunned by Rod's outburst to ask any more questions. He hung his head in defeat, not knowing what to do or say next. "No further questions, Your Honor."

Rod stepped down from the witness chair, and the clerk called Clara Marshall to the stand.

Troy looked from Mrs. Marshall to Rod, who stared back with a sly smirk. Rod's mother hadn't testified at the first trial. *Will the jury believe her new evidence?* he wondered.

After being sworn in, Clara Marshall hesitantly took her seat. She was nervous; she didn't want to be there but felt she needed to—for Rod's sake. She had always liked Troy. She and Mary had been the best of friends in years past. Her eyes met Mary's and, momentarily, she felt the temptation to step down and return to her seat. But then, thoughts of her little girl, her sweet little Jessica, filled her mind and heart with fresh grief. Someone had to pay for the crime. Since it was doubtful Colby would ever be caught and brought to trial, that *someone* had to be Troy.

Troy was so emotionally overwhelmed by the tears streaming down Clara's face it was hard to focus on what she said. The only part that stood out to him was her statement proclaiming she had seen him fire the gun. He knew it wasn't true, yet she sat there and firmly asserted that she had seen him murder her daughter.

When it was his turn, Troy considered declining to question her. Rod's mother had suffered more than any mother should. Yet, leaving her testimony intact would mean certain death for him and continued, unending anguish for his own mother.

"Mrs. Marshall," he began. He looked at her pale, tear-streaked face and his heart melted. He detested what he was about to attempt—to discredit her word. He took a deep breath, then started again. "Mrs. Marshall, I don't want to do this. I'd rather not ask you any questions, ma'am, but—"

"Because you know her testimony will put a rope around your neck," Rod mumbled.

"That will be your last comment from the audience, young man," the judge scolded him. "Continue, Mr. Daniels."

"Thank you, sir." Troy swallowed hard. "Mrs. Marshall, the only light in the room was from the moon shining through the window. I'm not sure how you could say, with certainty, that I fired the gun. I know you've been overcome with grief—"

Clara began sobbing.

"I object, your honor," cried Mr. James as he stood flailing his arm in the air. "The defendant is trying to make the witness seem unfit to testify!"

"I was just trying to establish that her grief may have caused her to ..." The word "lie" was on the tip of his tongue, but seeing her agony, he couldn't bring himself to verbalize it. He knew it would seal his doom, but he shook his head sadly and muttered, "No further questions, Your Honor."

Mary gasped! She looked at Clara, her eyes pleading with her to vindicate Troy.

Clara bit down on her lip, turning her face away as she rose from the witness seat and took her place next to Rod. Rod took her hand in his and gave her a reassuring nod. She rested her head on his shoulder and wept.

Troy was about to sit when the clerk called him to the witness stand. His heart began pounding. He ran his hand over his face, then numbly obeyed. His inward reaction to the dire situation was strange. It was as if he were encountering Rod's cold glares, the sickening sneer from Rachel's father, the devastated look on Clara Marshall's face, and the wide-eyed interest of the audience—most wishing, hoping for his defeat and execution. Yet, simultaneously, it was as if he were a spectator at the event, calmly watching the proceedings—confident that it would not affect him no matter the outcome. He was above the situation, and his mother and Rachel's comforting, supporting glances confirmed the latter part of his paradoxical emotions.

"Do you swear to tell the truth, the whole truth, and nothing but the truth, so help you, God?"

Troy spoke softly, still shaken from questioning Rod's mother. "Yes, sir."

"State your name," Mr. James demanded.

"Troy Daniels."

"State your father's name."

Troy looked the lawyer in the eyes. He knew the man was trying to bully him since the answer was already known. He had difficulty saying it aloud—of getting himself to admit to everyone who his father was. It was a name he wished he'd never heard, had never possessed as part of his own. "Colby—Colby Daniels."

"Colby Daniels. Colby Daniels," the lawyer repeated as he paced back and forth in front of Troy. "*The* Colby Daniels, otherwise known as 'Killer Colby?'"

The room was silent—deathly silent. The question was one he wished he didn't have to answer honestly. The years of disgrace living in the shadow of the man who robbed others of their livelihood, killed innocent people with no sense of guilt, and disregarded his own flesh and blood, seemed like an enormous weight crushing his spirit.

"Perhaps you didn't hear the question."

"I heard it!" Troy retorted. He hung his head as color flamed in his cheeks. "Yes, sir! Killer Colby is my pa."

The lawyer continued questioning Troy, exposing every minute detail of that terrible night. Troy answered methodically as if his answers were memorized. He had been through the story so many times—verbally, mentally, and emotionally.

"So you insist you did not pull the trigger on the gun that snuffed out the life of young Jessica Marshall?"

"Yes, sir. I—I tried to stop the shooting."

"Oh?" the lawyer said in a skeptical voice. "Now you're the *hero* instead of the guilty party?"

"I never *was* guilty, sir," Troy said flatly once the ensuing flurry of excited discussion among the spectators ceased.

"No criminal ever was," Mr. James added under his breath.

"Strike that from the record," the judge stated emphatically. "Mr. James, you will limit your words to questions only. You are not to interject your opinion or commentary."

"Of course, Your Honor," Mr. James replied, content that he had already planted a negative seed thought in the mind of the jurors.

"Will you tell the court who *did* kill Jessica Marshall?"

Troy hesitated, forcing himself to look directly at Rod. He tried to put himself in his former friend's place, to imagine the anger, resentment, and revenge that burned within his soul—the feelings of loss, grief, and turmoil tearing his family apart. Suddenly, he no longer saw Rod as an enemy but as a friend to be pitied, comforted, and consoled.

"Mr. Daniels," Judge Taylor admonished, "please answer the question."

Troy closed his eyes, visualizing once again the scene of the crime. He envisioned the large, rounded staircase in the dimly lit foyer of the Marshall home. Jessica, dressed in a white nightgown, was descending the stairs. He saw himself grabbing his father's arm, trying to wrestle the gun away as Colby raised his revolver and took aim. He heard the shot ...

"Mr. Daniels!"

Troy jumped at the sound of the judge's voice. Breathing heavily, his face white as a sheet, he sat silently as if stunned, then finally uttered the answer, "My pa, Colby Daniels."

The moment of agony passed quickly as the court session erupted into chaos and panic when three masked men stormed into the room.

"This trial is now over!" one of them shouted.

Recognizing the voice, Mary gasped when she turned around and saw him. "Colby!"

"No one tries to stop us, and no one gets hurt! Come with me, Troy!"

Troy was horrified; he couldn't move or speak.

"I said, 'Come with me, boy!'"

"No, Pa."

Colby cocked his gun and waved it around at the crowd. Women shrieked. Husbands clutched their wives closer. Mr. Wagner took Rachel's hand as he glared at Troy, ruing the day the young man showed interest in his daughter, wishing he had stopped the relationship. Clara Marshall burst into fresh tears.

"Ya do like I tell ya, or some of these people are gonna die."

Troy rose slowly from his chair and started walking toward his father. He didn't want to be responsible for anyone's injury or death, particularly that of his mother or Rachel.

Mary stood abruptly and grabbed his arm, trying to hold him back. "No, Troy! Please!"

"Mama, I have no choice," he said, shaking her off. A glint of steel from the back of the room caught Troy's eye. "No!" he shouted, running and throwing himself in front of his father just as a shot was fired. Troy cried out in pain, then fell in a heap on the floor.

The event caught Colby off guard, giving the sheriff time to knock the gun from his hand and take him into custody. Colby's accomplices escaped through the side door but were cut down by gunfire in the street as they tried to mount their horses.

Instantaneously, Mary and Rachel rushed to Troy's side. Mary drew her son's limp body to herself, rocking back and forth while she cradled him in her arms. Rachel grasped one of his hands and pressed it to her face and lips.

"Please," Mary cried, "someone get the doctor! Please!"

CHAPTER 18

Missing

Troy awoke to searing pain in his left side and the pungent smell of ether. A coarse handkerchief was being held over his nose and mouth. His eyes were wide with fear; he felt like he was being suffocated. Flailing his arms, he struggled against the firm hands, one holding the cloth to his face, the other holding his head still.

"Hold him down," the doctor's voice ordered.

Through glazed eyes, Troy saw a blurred vision of the sheriff leaning over him, pinning his arms against the rigid wooden operating table.

No! The plea sounded in his brain but failed to materialize on his lips as the repulsive odor permeated his nostrils.

"Don't fight it, boy," Doc Caldor said gently. "I know you don't understand what's happening, but it's for your own good. You've got a bullet lodged near your heart. I've got to get it out, or we'll lose you."

Troy tried forcefully tossing his head to the side, vainly striving to remove the overpowering smell. He tensed his muscles, straining to free his arms from the sheriff's powerful grip.

"Just calm down, son," the doctor continued. "We're trying to help you. Breathe deeply. Just a few more breaths."

Troy's brain became immersed in a dense fog. He could hear voices and see faces, but they seemed distant. It was as if he were in another world. The stinging in his chest was gone. His muscles relaxed. His breathing became slow and rhythmic.

The doctor looked at the sheriff. "He's a fighter!"

"Hopefully, it will help him win this battle," Mark commented, releasing Troy's limp arms.

"And then what?" the doctor whispered. "Perhaps it would be more humane to let him die now."

Mark shook his head. "With his father in custody, Troy has a better chance of being found innocent than before. What I'm concerned about are the two other men from Colby's gang, if they're even around here."

"What do you mean?"

"Troy told me there were four men in his pa's gang. We saw two today—those shot and killed outside the church. If Colby's entire gang came with him to Spring River, at least two more outlaws could be on the loose. And, no doubt, they'll be returning."

"Do you think they'll try to spring Colby from jail?" Doc Caldor asked as he thoroughly cleaned Troy's wound.

"Wouldn't surprise me if they did."

"Hand me that scalpel."

An assortment of sterilized surgical tools, bandages, and antiseptics had been laid on a clean white cloth atop a narrow, tall side table. Mark picked up the knife and handed it to the doctor.

"I'm surprised you're here and not guarding our infamous prisoner," Doc quipped as he made a neat incision to slightly enlarge the hole in Troy's chest, making it easier to reach in with his forceps and retrieve the bullet.

"I put Jeffrey Picketts in charge. He's a better shot than me, anyway." The sheriff grinned, remembering the turkey shoot contest the previous fall and how Jeffrey had bested him. He's stationing men outside the jail and on the outskirts of the town—all of them good shots. He's also sending riders to warn all the ranchers in the area to be on the lookout."

"What about the boy? You think he's innocent?"

Mark glanced down at Troy's pale face. "He can't hear us, can he?"

"No. No," the doctor assured him, "he can't hear what we're saying."

"Well, just between you and me—yes, I think he's innocent." Though outwardly needing to appear impartial, Mark admired Troy and his family. He didn't think the young man had committed the terrible crime he'd been accused of; it just didn't fit his personality. Troy had character; the whole family did, except for the father. Prisoners he'd dealt with in the past were the opposite.

"I also told Jeffrey to put some men outside your office," Mark informed the doctor. "Though, I'm more concerned about that Rod fellow trying to do Troy harm than I am about Colby's gang trying to take him out of here."

"He's definitely got the cards stacked against him."

There was a frantic knock at the door.

"Sheriff! Sheriff!" The voice was intense.

"It's Mary. Do you need me to stay, doc?"

"No, thanks. Once I finish up, I'll be strapping him to the bed while he's still asleep. That way, when he wakes up, he won't be able to move and bust the stitches open."

Mark nodded, then opened the door. Mary's face was almost as pale as Troy's. "What is it, Mary? What's happened?"

Mary's eyes diverted from the sheriff to the table in the middle of the room—where Troy lay still as death. She put her hand over her mouth and gasped. "He's not—"

Mark shut the door behind him. "No, Mary. He's asleep so Doc can get the bullet out."

"He's going to be all right, isn't he? I can't lose him! I can't lose them both!"

"What do you mean, both? Troy and Colby?"

"No, Angie. Please, please help me find her!" Mary burst into tears.

"Sit down," Mark said, gently leading her to a chair in the doctor's waiting room. "What's happened?"

"She's gone! I went back to the mercantile after Troy was brought here. She'd been staying there during the trial. I left her with Pop. He's been so despondent since Mom passed—just sits in a chair all day long, staring, with a blank look on his face. Besides, I didn't want her to hear the nasty things people would say about Troy. I didn't want her to see her brother go through that," Mary rambled. "But I shouldn't have left her. It's all my fault! I thought she'd be safe. I've looked everywhere! No one's seen her!"

"You think she wandered off somewhere?"

"I don't know. It's not like her to do something like that. I told her to stay put. I ..."

A troubling thought passed through the sheriff's mind. *Colby's men. What if they'd taken the girl? Maybe that's how they planned on getting Colby released—by doing an exchange.*

"What is it?" Mary asked, noticing his furrowed brows and the deep concern in his eyes.

Mark shook his head. "Everything will be all right," he mumbled, trying to convince himself as much as Mary that his quest to find Angie would succeed.

Not wanting to waste time, he questioned Pop first since he had been the last to see her. "Pop," Mark said, looking directly into the old man's vacant eyes. "Pop, you have to think back to when Angie was with you. It was just today, not more than a few hours ago. Do you remember?"

"Angie?" Pop repeated as if he'd never heard the name before.

Mary took Jeremy's hand and bent down to talk to him as he sat in his rocker by the window overlooking the street below. "Pop, it's Mary. I know you've been through a trying time, but you must

116

think back to when Angie was with you. It was just this morning. Please, please try to remember."

There was no response. Mary brushed away a tear and glanced up at the sheriff.

Mark shook his head sadly. "It's no use. We'll have to start with something or someone else."

Mary nodded. "Pop," she said, gently caressing his hand. "It's all right. It will come to you. When it does, you can tell me. All right? We have to leave now, but I'll fix you some supper later on." She gave him a sympathetic look, patted his hand, then stood up.

"Don't worry, Mary," Mark assured her once they'd descended the stairs into the store. "I'll find her."

They walked together in silence until they reached the front of the mercantile.

"Can you give me something that belongs to your daughter?" Mark asked. "Anything—like a piece of clothing. Wilbur Tremont owns the Bar T Ranch just out of town. He has a pair of excellent hunting dogs. They should be able to follow her scent."

"I hope so." Mary sighed as she disappeared into her family's little room and started rummaging through the dresser drawers. *I don't want to give the sheriff anything large like a skirt or dress. Angie only owns a couple and will need them when she comes home.* Mary slumped against the dresser. *If she comes home,* she thought. The tears came unbidden as she rested her elbows on the dresser, releasing the pent-up emotions consuming her.

"Mary, is everything all right?" Mark asked quietly. When he didn't receive an answer, he walked into the room. "Mary?"

"I'm sorry," she said, sniffing back the tears. "I can't—I can't ..."

Mark gently turned her toward himself and let her cry on his shoulder. Then, hesitatingly, he placed a comforting arm around her until she calmed down.

"I'm sorry," she said, embarrassed by her actions and pulling away from him. "I just got overwhelmed."

"There's nothing to be sorry about," he replied. "It's totally understandable."

Mary turned back to the dresser. "I think there's a scarf of hers in here somewhere," she muttered, haphazardly moving things about in her search. "It's blue—her favorite color. Here! Here it is." She turned back to the sheriff and handed it to him. "Do you think that will be enough?"

"Should be. Did she wear it recently?"

"Yes. Just yesterday."

"It's perfect." He placed a hand on her shoulder. "Mary, I'll find her. I promise. She's going to be fine."

Mary nodded her agreement, though her mind continued to plague her with negative thoughts of Troy dying from a bullet wound or being hanged and Angie never coming back, at least not alive.

"You and your children have great faith in God," Mark said. "Hang on to that faith, Mary. Hang on to it with everything you have!"

She sniffed back tears and nodded again, then gazed into his eyes with a haunted, pleading look. "Please, please don't let anyone tell Troy about Angie. He needs to get well. I don't want anything to upset him." She turned away from Mark. "He has enough to be concerned about." Her hand went up to her mouth as she stifled a gasp.

"For what it's worth," Mark said, going against his better judgment of not showing partiality, "I believe Troy is innocent. I plan on being a witness for him when, if, his trial resumes."

"Then you think he'll still need to go through with that? What if Colby is found guilty?"

"It's true. That could change everything for Troy—unless the judge decides differently."

Mary's eyes welled up with tears again.

Realizing he'd spoken hastily and added to her angst, Mark said, "Even if the trial continues, I don't think he'll hang. At least—not if I can help it.

"Why don't you rest for a while? The store can stay closed for now. I'll see if someone can help with it tomorrow, so you won't need to manage it." He shifted his eyes to the ceiling. "Pop's in no shape to do anything, and you have enough to deal with. I'll send someone over to stay with him as well."

"You're so kind, Sheriff. Thank you."

Mark tipped his hat to her. "Promise me you'll rest and not worry."

"But, Troy—"

"There's nothing you can do for him right now. The doc has everything under control. Everything will be all right," he said soothingly, all the while wondering how his words could ever come true. "Get some rest."

"I'll try."

"Oh," Mark added before heading out the door, "and pray, Mary. I've never been a praying man, but—I'll pray, too."

Mary smiled weakly as the sheriff left with the scarf.

CHAPTER 19

Uncertain Times

T roy woke up with a start, then clutched at the linen sheets covering his fevered body. He grit his teeth against the sharp, cutting twinge that knifed through his chest.

Closing his eyes, he laid back for a few moments as the agony subsided, replaced by a burning that engulfed him. He tried concentrating on the tick-tock, tick-tock of the mantel clock in the unfamiliar room. The pulsating pain near his left shoulder returned, taking on a rhythmic relationship with the timepiece until they blended into one.

A sudden shuffling of feet across the floor roused him back into reality. He became aware of his labored breathing, realizing he was starting to give in to his affliction and death was fighting to consume him. He wanted to welcome it as one would receive an old friend, reach out for it and grasp it lovingly by the hand, for death held nothing but peace and deliverance. And, yet, he knew he must fight for his life, no matter how long that life would be—a few minutes, a few hours, a few days—for someone else's life depended on it, someone else's eternal soul.

With a pained expression, Troy lifted his heavy eyelids and focused his hot, itching eyes on Doctor Caldor. "Doc," he muttered weakly, "am I ... going to ... make it?"

"I'll be honest with you, son. I don't know. I'd say you have a fifty-fifty chance."

"I ... have to make it. My mother ... needs me. Angie ... needs me. Rachel ..." He closed his eyes and fell back to sleep.

When he awoke again in five hours, he looked up at Rachel. "I must be dreaming," he murmured weakly.

"No, Troy." She bent down and kissed his forehead. "You're not dreaming."

"Your father ... let you come?"

"Yes. I know—it's a miracle. The doctor talked to him. He said it would be good if those closest to you came to see you."

"I'm surprised your father ... wants me to live." He closed his eyes and grimaced as the throbbing discomfort returned.

"Oh, Troy. Father doesn't hate you."

Troy sighed. "I wish I could ... believe that. What about Mama? Angie? Are they ... here, too?"

Rachel swallowed the lump in her throat. She had visited briefly with Mary and learned of Angie's disappearance. Her promise to keep the news from Troy was a sacred trust. "Not right now. Just me."

"Just you. What more ... could I ask for?" Another wave of deep, stinging torment—his mouth contorted into a twisted smile as a low moan escaped his lips. He tried reaching for her hand. "I—I can't lift ... my arm. Rachel, I can't lift my arm!" Panicking, he tried sitting up but couldn't. "I'm paralyzed!"

"Shh," she said calmly, stroking his hair. "It's all right, Troy. You're not paralyzed. You're strapped to the bed. The doctor feared you'd try to get up, and the bleeding would start again. So, just relax and try not to move. You're supposed to keep as still as possible." She moved the covers back slightly on his right side, pulled a chair beside the bed, then took his hand. "Do you feel my hand on yours?"

"Yes," he replied, relaxing his muscles.

The two remained quiet for a few moments, each thinking of the other, longing for a future together and afraid it would never be.

"My ... my pa, is he—"

"He's in jail. His trial starts tomorrow."

"He's guilty, Rachel. Guilty of Jessica's ... death, guilty of so many things. I'm not sure ... why I took that bullet for him except that, all ... of a sudden, I cared about his soul. Why would I care? After all the ... terrible things he's done. Why should I care?"

"Perhaps God put *His* love for your father in your heart."

"He'll hang, Rachel. He'll hang ... for sure. Then he'll go to ... I have to talk to him!" Troy struggled against the ropes holding him fast.

"No, Troy, don't! Don't!

"Doctor!"

She sprang from her seat and rushed to the door. "Please, help me!" she pleaded with the two men stationed there for Troy's protection. "He's trying to get up! He needs to stay still. Where's the doctor?"

"He went to the café for a bite to eat."

"Please, hold him still until I get back."

The men nodded and rushed into the room as Troy struggled to free himself.

"You take his arms. I'll get his legs," one of them said to the other.

"Hold still, boy. Hold still. The doctor will be here in a few minutes."

Troy heard words, but his brain couldn't understand their meaning. "Let me go! Let me go! I'm innocent! Please ... please don't hang me!"

Just then, Doc Caldor rushed in, wiping the crumbs of the blueberry cobbler he'd just enjoyed from his mouth. "I've got to give him something to put him out for a while. Otherwise, he'll tear the stitches open." At that moment, the doctor noticed blood seeping from Troy's wound, staining the sheet. He rushed to get his supplies and soon had ether back over Troy's nose. "Hold him tight!" the doc ordered.

"No! Don't ... suffocate me!" Troy thrashed his head back and forth, trying to escape the overpowering fumes. "Please! Please!"

"Rachel, come hold his head still. Rachel ..." A loud thud on the floor caught the attention of all three men. Rachel had fainted.

The doctor sighed. "At least she didn't crash into the cabinet. It would have been a much harder fall. I'll tend to her in a minute. But, first, I have to get him sedated."

Troy's breathing became steady again; his arms and legs went limp. Doc Caldor checked to see that he was still breathing, then left his patient momentarily and bent down to check on Rachel. "She has a small lump on her head. I think she'll be fine. Lay her on the bed in the next room. I'll be there as soon as I can. I have to restitch Troy first before he loses any more blood. There's no time to lose. It may already be too late."

CHAPTER 20

In God's Hands

W hen Rachel awoke, her father was standing over her. "Rachel," he said, his voice mirroring the relief he felt. "Rachel, honey, I was so worried about you."

"What happened?"

"You fainted."

"Troy! What happened to Troy?" she asked, frantically trying to raise herself from the bed.

Mr. Wagner placed a hand on each shoulder, gently keeping her down. "The doctor said you were to be as still as possible."

"But, Troy? Is he all right? Is he still alive?"

Her father took one hand away and scratched the back of his neck. It irritated him that she cared about the young man. Part of his frustration was that Troy was still alive; it would have been easier if the bullet had taken him. He felt guilty having such thoughts and knew Rachel wouldn't understand what he was about to say, but he needed to do what was best for her. "He's still alive, but you're to have nothing more to do with him."

"Father," Rachel could hardly believe what she was hearing, "you said I could go see him."

"Yes, I did. You had your chance, and—look what happened! I'm not going to risk your health for his." His condescending tone conveyed the contempt he held for Troy.

"Father, he's innocent. You know he's innocent. Now that they've captured his pa—"

"It doesn't prove a thing. Troy admitted to being at the Marshall's house when Jessica was shot."

"But that doesn't mean he killed her." She spoke earnestly but respectfully. She loved her father and didn't want to unnecessarily drive a wedge between them, although she knew it was already there. It had started when he first discovered she was interested in Troy. The gap that had little by little widened between them had grown into an uncrossable chasm when Troy was first arrested. Now, it appeared there was no possibility of building a bridge.

Rachel sighed and settled back against her pillow. Her head throbbed; her heart ached. There was nothing more she could do but leave her future in God's hands.

CHAPTER 21

The Search

M ark rode out to Wilbur Tremont's ranch.

"I need your help, Wilbur. There's a little girl who's gone missing. I need to borrow your dogs."

"Jed and Riley? Sure thing. You got somethin' for them to smell?"

Mark dismounted, then held up the scarf. "This."

Wilbur nodded. "Follow me, Sheriff. They're out in the barn. Who is this little girl? Must be someone I know."

Mark answered cautiously, not knowing on which side of the trial Wilbur stood. "She's—the sister of the Daniels boy, Colby Daniel's little girl."

"Hmph! Can't imagine an outlaw havin' a little girl—not one worth savin' anyways. Children usually follow in their parents' footsteps, just like that Troy fellow."

Mark locked eyes with him, shocked that someone he'd known all his life, someone with five children of his own, could be so calloused. "For one thing, Wilbur, Troy hasn't been found guilty."

"Not yet, at least."

"For another—from what I understand, this little girl, Angie, never even met her pa. She's been raised by Mrs. Daniels, a good Christian woman. The girl's only seven years old, Wilbur. About the age of your Sarah. Try to think how it would be for you and Melonie if someone kidnapped *your* daughter!"

"I didn't say I wouldn't help," Wilbur remarked. "I just said I didn't think a thief and murderer could have decent offspring. They've got bad blood flowing through their veins."

Mark shook his head in disbelief. "Bad blood," he muttered under his breath.

"But when you bring up the fact they was mostly raised by their ma, that changes things a bit," Wilbur was quick to add. "Still—the boy had some doin's with his pa, or he wouldn't have been at the Marshall place that night."

"The trial never got far enough along for Troy to testify that he was forced to go."

"Forced to go? Is that what he told you?"

"Yes."

Wilbur was skeptical. "And you believe him?"

Mark nodded in the affirmative. "Yes. Yes, I do."

"I'm surprised you'd be so gullible."

"I'm not being gullible. I've been sheriff for over ten years now. I've dealt with lots of lowlifes. Troy doesn't fit the pattern." Mark tipped his hat back out of his face. "The boy told me there were four men with his pa. Two of them were shot outside the church. I'm afraid the other two may have kidnapped the girl."

"You think they'll try to make a trade?"

"That's exactly what I think. We must find her and get her safely away from them before they can carry out their plan."

The two arrived at the barn. As if sensing they were needed, Wilbur's bloodhounds came around the side of the building to greet them, barking and shivering with excitement to have a visitor.

"How many men do you have to help look?" Wilbur asked.

"Just me, I'm afraid," Mark answered. "I've got all the able-bodied men I know taking turns stationed at different places throughout the town—just in case Colby's men show up. I've warned them not to shoot if the girl is with them. I can't take much time, but I promised Mrs. Daniels I'd find her daughter."

I can spare an hour or two," Wilbur said thoughtfully. "I'll go with you. Just let me saddle up. The dogs will listen to me better than you, anyway."

"I more than appreciate that, Wilbur." Mark mounted his steed. "I didn't think I'd have any help. Thank you."

Wilbur nodded and disappeared into the barn, returning soon with his quarter horse.

"I think we should head back into town," Mark said, "and start where she was before being abducted."

"Maybe she just wandered off, and she's home safe and sound."

"I hope that's the case, but her mother says it wouldn't be like her. No, Wilbur, I have a bad feeling about this."

The two rode out with the dogs bounding close behind.

When they arrived at the mercantile, Wilbur dismounted. "Hand me that there scarf, Sheriff."

Mark gave him the wrap. Wilbur crouched down as Jed and Riley, tails wagging, came over to him. "Take a good whiff, boys," Wilber said. "Now—find!" Quickly, Wilbur mounted his horse, and they were off.

Hearing voices, Mary looked out the little front window of her family's room and watched until the men and dogs disappeared from view. "Oh, Lord," she said audibly, leaning her weary head against the window pane. "Please, please let them find Angie! And please, let Troy be all right!"

Mary had rested for only a half-hour but knew she couldn't sleep anymore. She needed to see Troy as soon as possible—to hold one of her children close.

129

CHAPTER 22

Dead End

Wilbur's dogs followed Angie's scent with a fury, sniffing and grunting furiously at the ground, the air, and nearby bushes. Mark followed the dogs and discovered the faint tracks of several horses' hooves. Since it hadn't rained in nearly a week, they could have belonged to anyone recently coming in or out of Spring River. The dogs darted to the right, where the road forked outside the town. The horse tracks dwindled to just two, then ended about a mile away at the edge of the woods.

"They're headin' to the river," Wilbur noted.

"I'm afraid so," Mark admitted. "Looks like Colby and his men planned things out ahead of time. Let's follow until your dogs lose the scent."

Wilbur nodded and gently nudged his horse on with his heels.

It was as they had suspected. Upon reaching the edge of Spring River, the dogs lost all traces of Angie. Prancing around in circles, they ventured to the water's edge, backed up, sniffed the ground, then repeated the sequence. Finally, exhausted from their futile activity, the two lay down and whimpered their disgust at having failed their mission.

Mark surveyed the river from his perch on his Appaloosa. "The river's only about two to three feet deep along this entire stretch. I'm guessing they went straight in, then, about halfway, turned to the left or right and came out on the other side farther down or up the line into the woods."

Wilbur nodded in agreement. "It could take hours to find the tracks."

Mark sighed. "You've got a good point. We could cross here, then split up. We'll look for tracks along the riverbank on the other side and signal to each other if we find something. Of course, if they're smart, they'll be covering their tracks, so there may be nothing to see."

"It's worth a try."

"Absolutely. Let's go, and keep your rifle ready, Wilbur. They could be hiding in the trees. I'm sure they must assume we're looking for them."

Mark and Wilbur returned to town several hours later—without Angie.

"I'm real sorry things didn't work out, Sheriff," Wilbur said. I'd like to help more, but I'm goin' to Laramie tomorrow to buy some cattle. Takin' some of my hands with me."

"That's all right, Wilbur," Mark added. "Colby's trial starts tomorrow, so most of my time will be taken up in court. But I'll figure out something," Mark added, wondering what that would be.

Wilbur tipped his hat and headed back to his ranch, Jed and Riley barking and leaping about his horse with renewed energy after their relaxing nap by the water's edge.

Mark sighed and opened the door to the mercantile.

"Did you find her?" Emma Tucker whispered to him from behind the counter.

Mark shook his head sadly. "Is Mary in the room?"

"She's upstairs with Pop. Sally took sick, so Mary said she'd take her place. Such a giving person that Mary Daniels. Such a shame she married that Colby fellow. Makes a body wonder how such a sweet woman ended up with the likes of him!"

Mark nodded and headed to the back of the shop, then up the stairs. He hesitated for a moment before knocking. *This isn't going to be easy,* he thought. *How can I break the news to her?*

Mary answered the door. "Sheriff, did you find her?"

The look on his face already conveyed the answer. "I'm sorry, Mary. I—I don't know what to say except I'm not giving up."

Mary put a hand up to her eye and whisked away an unbidden tear. "I haven't stopped praying for her. God knows where she is. I must trust Him to keep her safe. It's not easy." A few more tears escaped and trickled down her face.

Mark felt helpless. He wanted to assure her that everything would be fine in the end, but he had no way of knowing that and didn't want to give her false hope. "I'll look for her every chance I get, Mary."

Mary nodded and wiped her face with the handkerchief she had pulled from her apron pocket.

"Any improvement in Pop?" Mark asked, hoping the change in conversation would be beneficial.

Mary opened the door for Mark to see inside the room. Pop was still rocking slowly in the chair, staring blankly out at the road below.

Mark sighed, then turned to leave. "The good news is," he said, glancing back at Mary before heading down the stairs, "if the outlaws are planning on exchanging your daughter for Colby like I think they will, they won't do anything to harm her."

Mary forced a smile. "Thank you for trying, Sheriff." She shut the door, then leaned against it, tears coursing down her face. She felt like every ounce of strength was being sapped from her body. *Oh, Lord,* she pleaded inwardly, *please ... please ... help!*

CHAPTER 23

Not Tomorrow

Mark felt guilty. After the futile attempt he and Wilbur had made, no one was left to help search for Angie. As sheriff, Mark needed to be present at Colby's trial, giving him just a few daylight hours each day to continue looking. Over and over, he warned the men guarding the town not to fire if there were a little girl with the outlaws.

Mary spent her waking hours by Troy's side—for her benefit as much as his. Holding his hand, praying, bathing his brow with cool water, and telling him how much she loved him was therapy for both. She never told him about his sister's desperate situation nor allowed anyone else to mention it in his presence. Whenever he asked why Angie didn't come to see him, Mary assured him he could visit with her once he was healed, hoping against hope that her words would prove true. There was another advantage to staying close to Troy. As much as she despised her son's situation, she was glad for an excuse not to attend Colby's trial.

Little by little, Troy regained his strength. The doctor said Troy was lucky. The bullet had lodged near his heart; one half-inch closer would have drastically changed the outcome. Mary and Troy knew it wasn't luck. It was the grace of God.

The day finally came when Troy was well enough to leave the doctor's office.

"I'm sorry, son," Mark said. "I have to take you back to jail until the judge declares you innocent."

"Do you think he will, sir? I mean, my trial never really ended. And, my pa admitted that he committed the crime—right?"

"Yes, that's right."

"So, will I still have to be tried?"

"I'm not exactly sure what the judge has in mind, Troy. I'm just following orders. But don't you fret. I don't think you have anything to worry about."

Troy shuddered involuntarily as he and the sheriff walked past the gallows being constructed in the center of town.

"I'm putting you in the cell next to your pa, Troy."

"I don't mind being in the same cell with him, Sheriff."

"It's for your safety, son. You're still healing up, and he's one angry man. You can talk to him through the bars."

"Whatever you say, sir."

"You give a holler if you need me," Mark said as he turned the key in the lock on the metal door.

"Thank you, sir. I will."

The sheriff left the room, locking the adjoining wooden door behind him. He hid the keys in his office in a small glass jar behind the pot-bellied stove in the corner. Now that Colby's trial was over and his hanging imminent, Mark was sure the outlaw's gang would make their move—soon. It made him uneasy and tense. He had two men stationed in front of the jail's outer door, two by the cell windows and one on the roof.

He had hope that Angie was still alive. *Colby's men will need her to get Colby out,* he assured himself. *I have so many stationed around the town's perimeter there's no way they'll sneak into town without us knowing.* But then, a troubling thought rattled his brain. *What if they try something at the hanging? Everyone will be out in the open.*

Colby stood in front of the small barred window. "Ya'll have a good view of the hangin' there from your cell. It's tomorrow, in case yer wantin' to know."

"I know," Troy answered simply.

Colby looked over at his son. "Guess that won't disappoint ya none, will it?"

Troy studied his pa's vacant eyes set deep within the rough, ruddy face etched with deep lines. The mouth, thin and tight, covered any emotion that may have struggled within the cold-blooded heart. He followed the scar from the left corner of his pa's mouth to the tip of his left ear, ending just beneath tousled shocks of tawny-brown hair. "I won't be watching."

"Yer Mama will probably be there. I bet she can hardly wait till she's got rid of me," Colby sputtered bitterly.

"I don't think she'll be watching either."

"No? She only come to see me once since I've been here."

Troy was amazed his mother had come at all or that the calloused man before him would have expected it. "It's been hard for her, Pa."

"She told me she'd forgiven me for everythin' I've ever done. Now weren't that nice of her?" He snickered.

Troy was angry. "You're going to die tomorrow, and you still—"

"Still what, boy?"

"Still have no remorse for ruining her life, the lives of your children, for all the money you've stolen, the lies you've told, the people you've hurt—"

"And killed, boy! Don't forget that!"

A haunted look passed over Troy's face as his mind pictured once again the moment Jessica fell to the floor. "No, sir, I won't forget that. I can't."

137

An awkward silence ensued as Colby nervously paced the floor for a few minutes. "That was a fool thing ya done, boy, runnin' between me and that gun." He shook his head. "I wonder if that fellow who shot ya got reward money fer both of us." He paused, waiting for a response from Troy, which never came. "Anyway, I still can't figure out why ya tried to save my life. What if ya'd died, boy? What if ya'd died fer a worthless creature like me? Now that would have been somethin' fer yer Mama to deal with. The innocent fer the guilty."

"I was ready to die. You weren't. You're still not ready. I hoped it would give you another chance to repent, but ..." The urgency Troy felt in his soul spilled over into his voice. "You're gonna be in Hell tomorrow!"

"Oh, that's right," Colby said sarcastically. "Yer goin' to Heaven when ya die, and I'm goin' to Hell. Ya go right ahead and condemn yer pa. Yer 'Mr. Do-Right'. Ya didn't want nothin' to do with my kind of life." He spat on the floor, then spoke with disdain. "Always been a coward, haven't ya, Troy, tied to yer Mama's apron strings!"

Troy found what he'd just heard to be incredulous. "I purposely—purposely took that bullet for you, and you call me a coward? No, I didn't want anything to do with your kind of life, but not because I'm a coward." He softened his tone. "And not because I'm perfect. I'm as much a sinner as you are."

"Oh really? And how do ya figure that?"

"The Bible says, 'For all have sinned and come short of the glory of God.' Sin is sin. There's not one person on earth who hasn't broken at least one of God's laws. Besides, the Bible tells us we're born sinners, separated from God's holiness because of our sin."

"I'm warnin' ya, Troy," Colby said threateningly. "I don't want no Bible thrown in my face."

"If you don't let me tell you what the Bible says, there's no hope for you. None! It's God's Word that tells us how to escape Hell, how to have forgiveness for our sins, how to live a life that's pleasing to God, how we can be assured of Heaven when we die."

Troy moved close to the bars dividing the two cells. He looked his father in the eye and spoke earnestly. "Christians aren't people who think they're holier than everyone else. To become a Christian, you have to admit that you're so wicked you need a Savior."

Colby reached his left hand through the bars and grabbed the front of Troy's shirt. "I told ya to shut yer mouth, boy! The sheriff may think yer safe bein' on the other side of them bars, but I can still cause ya lots of pain. Ya know what my temper can be like! Don't push me!"

"You do what you want to me. You can't get out of here, and I'm gonna tell you about the Lord whether you want to hear about Him or not!"

Still holding Troy against the metal poles with his left hand, Colby thrust his right hand through an opening. Troy bent over in pain from the swift, brutal punch his father gave to his stomach. He stumbled over to the bed, then sat down.

"Don't you understand, Pa?" he said solemnly. "I'm tellin' you because I care about what happens to you! I don't want you to spend eternity in Hell!"

Colby walked over to the window, grasped one of the bars, and stared at the backs of the men guarding the jail. He knew he didn't deserve his son's concern; he didn't deserve the consideration of anyone. "Why should ya care about me?"

"Because you're my pa—"

Colby laughed disdainfully, "I ain't never been no kind of pa to ya. All I ever brung ya and yer Mama was grief. Are ya forgettin' the times I came home drunk and beat up on ya? The times ya went hungry because there was no food in the house? The shame of bein' called the son of Killer Colby?"

A jumbled collection of memories reared its ugly head again in Troy's mind. He was silent briefly as he thought back through the years. All the things his father said were true. Yet, the one thing that hadn't been mentioned came to the forefront—that his pa was mainly absent. The only connection he had to this man was physical—through blood. There was no emotional attachment.

None whatsoever. *It's a good question. Why should I care about Colby Daniels? I didn't care before—not until the moment I knew that bullet would take his life.*

The answer came almost immediately. *Because,* he told himself, *Jesus loves this pitiful excuse of a human. He loved him enough to die for his soul.*

"No, sir, I ain't forgetting. I hate the things you've done! But I love you because—because Christ died for you."

Colby shook his head. Troy's attitude made no sense to him, and neither did the fact that his son had taken a bullet meant for him. With all the evil he'd done in his lifetime, Colby only felt pangs of guilt initially. The more he'd robbed, killed, and stomped on the rights of others to please his selfish desires, the less his conscience had bothered him. It had become a way of life, a game to see if he could outsmart the law.

"You said if that bullet had killed me and I would have died in your place—it would have been the innocent for the guilty. Right?"

Colby said nothing.

"Jesus Christ truly was innocent. Yet, He willingly shed His blood and gave His life for the guilty. He was the only One Who could pay the penalty for our sin because He was the sinless Son of God."

Colby sighed. "I'm listenin', Troy."

"Jesus died for the sins of everyone who's ever lived, but His death only pays for our sins if we ask Him to forgive us. A man has to repent—be sorry for his sin, turn away from them—"

"And ya think yer pa's beyond that, don't ya? Ya think I ain't got no conscience, no sorrow fer the things I've done. Well, that's where yer wrong, Troy. A man can put on a tough front if ya know what I mean." The faces of those he'd wronged in the past—those whose lives he had ended, paraded before his mind. He started breathing heavily, the pent-up emotions of years of wickedness all but choking out his words. "But inside, he's being eaten away—eaten away by guilt, by memories, by his wretchedness."

"Then give it to Christ. Ask Him to forgive you."

"It's too late for that, Troy!"

140

"No!" Troy shouted. "*Tomorrow* will be too late! There's no chance to receive Christ after death."

"I'm beyond savin', Troy. I don't deserve God's forgiveness. Not after all I've done."

Troy came close to his father's cell again yet remained at a safe distance."None of us deserve God's forgiveness, Pa," he said gently, "but no one's beyond saving. The Bible says, 'Christ came to call sinners to repentance.' 'He came to seek and to save that which was lost.' 'While we were yet sinners, Christ died for us.' All you need to do is pray—"

"Sheriff! Sheriff!" Troy and Colby could hear the anxious shout from one of the men guarding the jail as he burst through the door to Mark's office.

"What is it, Justin?"

"It's them! They're here! And they've got the girl with them—that Angie."

Angie? Troy looked out the window. *Pa's men kidnapped Angie! No wonder I haven't heard from her or seen her. Everyone's kept it a secret from me.* He locked eyes with his father. "Your men took Angie?"

"I needed some security, boy—just in case I got caught. Looks like it paid off."

They could hear Mark yelling to the men stationed around town. "Hold your fire! Hold your fire!"

"How could you put your daughter in a place of danger?" Troy questioned angrily.

The key scraped inside the lock of the door that separated them from the sheriff's office. Mark entered, his shoulders sagging; he'd come close to ending Colby's reign of terror. So close. But now, he had to think of Mary's daughter. "All right, Daniels. Let's go," he said to Colby as he unlocked the cell, keeping his revolver trained on the outlaw. "I have more men in and outside my office, so don't try anything. I'm only doing this to rescue the girl."

Colby grinned as his attitude immediately changed to sarcasm. He had more time; no need to worry about his soul just yet. "Guess

I won't be goin' to Hell tomorrow after all," he sneered at Troy, mocking the concerned look on his son's face.

Troy shook his head in disbelief. He had thought his father would respond to the gospel. Colby had been just a prayer away from God's saving grace. *But,* Troy told himself, *if Pa could be swayed that quickly one way or the other, his "repentance" wasn't genuine.* He listened to the clang of the metal cell door and the thump of the wooden one, separating him forever from the man who had plagued his life.

He watched out his cell window. Across the street were two men dismounting from their horses. One lifted Angie from the saddle and set her on the ground. Troy was relieved that she seemed unharmed. Nevertheless, he wondered how the transfer would be done safely. Closing his eyes, he silently prayed for his sister's protection.

Townsfolk had gathered on the street at the first shouts of activity. Troy wondered if his mother had heard and if Toby was peaking his beady eyes over the window ledge inside his shop while safely hiding behind the wall.

"You people, go inside!" Mark ordered. He looked down the road to his left. Mary was standing outside the mercantile, her arms reaching out toward her daughter. "Go inside!" he shouted to her.

"I can't! I have to be sure Angie's all right," came the worried reply.

"Please, Mary, for your safety, do as I—"

"Tell your men to throw down their guns!" one of Colby's men demanded.

"Everyone," Mark yelled. "Put your guns down! We can't risk anything happening to the girl! Put them down!" he shouted again, seeing the stubbornness of a few who were unwilling to release their weapons.

"All right," he said to the two men. "They're unarmed, but I'm keeping my revolver on Colby until that little girl gets safely to me."

"Nothin' doin', Sheriff! We've got no guarantee we won't be shot once she's with you. Release Colby first!"

Troy watched in horror as Angie broke loose from her captors and ran toward the mercantile.

No, Angie! Troy's heart cried out. He lost sight of her but heard the shot one of the gang members fired. The bullet whizzed past her head, lodging in a wooden post on the front porch.

Mary grabbed her daughter's hand, pulling her inside. Shutting the door quickly, she ran with Angie in tow toward the back of the store and up the steps, the man who had fired at Angie following in pursuit.

Mark left his prisoner and ran as fast as he could toward the mercantile.

Colby saw his chance to escape. He ran across the street to one of the horses, put his foot in the stirrup, and hoisted himself onto the saddle. As he and the remaining gang member started riding away, shots volleyed from several places. Troy stood frozen at the cell window, hearing the loud ricochet of gunshots as he watched his pa and his accomplice fall onto the hard dirt road.

A few townsmen cautiously exited their posts, walked over to the still forms, and kicked them. "They're dead!" The words echoed back and forth between spectators as they rejoiced over the demise of the outlaws.

Troy turned and lowered himself slowly to the floor, his back against the wall. "Not tomorrow, Pa," he whispered hoarsely. "Today."

Meanwhile, Mary hastily wedged a chair under the doorknob inside Pop's apartment while Angie stood nearby, sobbing. They could hear the pounding of feet coming up the stairs. Mary held her breath, hoping the chair would hold. "Back away, Angie, in case he shoots. Back away!"

Two shots rang out—one from the top of the stairs, one from down in the shop! Another gunshot, then a scream, and the shattering of broken glass as the outlaw crashed through the stair's railing, landing on a shelf of dishes and toppling over with them to the floor. Mark cautiously walked over to the man, his gun smoking. The outlaw lay among the sharp fragments—lifeless.

Mark rushed up the stairs. "Mary! Mary! It's Sheriff Kirby. Are you and Angie all right?"

Mary clumsily removed the chair with her shaking hands and opened the door.

"Are you and Angie all right? You didn't get hurt, did you?" Mark asked breathlessly.

"We're fine," Mary said, her voice trembling, "but I've never been so scared!" She reached out to Angie and drew her close. "I was so scared!"

Mark placed a hand on her shoulder. "Take some deep breaths, Mary. It's over now. It's over."

"Is Colby—"

"I don't know. I came here right away. But I—I heard shots."

Mary nodded. She'd heard them, too, through Pop's open window, along with the rejoicing in the street. Although unable to decipher what was being said, she knew in her heart that Colby was gone.

CHAPTER 24

Toby's Threat

Mark left the burial of the two gang members up to the towns-folk. The men who'd guarded Spring River felt satisfaction and closure in protecting the town as they dug the graves far away in an isolated place next to the other two gang members who had previously been killed.

Colby's burial was different. Choosing a secret location and a nighttime interment, Mark decided it best to involve only the Daniels family and himself. That way, no one could harass Mary and her family during the burial. Bounty hunters or someone looking for easy money wouldn't be tempted to dig up the famous outlaw and claim the reward for his death in some other jurisdiction.

No one seemed to have a problem with the arrangement except Toby. The following day, he barged into Mark's office, fuming. "We was a part of bringin' down that lowlife, Sheriff. It ain't right you hidin' from everyone where he's buried. You've been mighty friendly all along with the criminal's family. I'm bringin' it up at the next town meetin'!"

"You do that, Toby," Mark said flatly.

"And what about that Troy fellow?" Toby gestured towards the next room.

"What about him?"

"He's still gonna be tried, ain't he? I mean, his pa may have admitted to the killin', but the boy was an accessory. Besides, it's our duty to clean up our town from any and all Daniels."

"You planning on hanging his mother and sister, too?" Mark questioned indifferently.

"Of course not! Just the boy. He was there at the crime. He as much as said so. We'll run the rest of his kinfolk out of town, is all. That's the only way Spring River can get back to normal."

"Maybe we should run you out of town while we're at it," Mark mumbled as he rummaged through the new wanted posters on his desk.

"How's that? What did you say?"

"Go home, Toby. Mind your own business."

"This *is* my business! Have you forgotten? I was a key witness at the boy's trial."

Mark glanced up at him. "You weren't a witness to anything."

"I want to see the boy."

"Sorry, the answer is, 'No.'"

"There you go again—protectin' the criminal."

"He's not a criminal until proven guilty."

"Then why is he still locked up? Tell me that!"

Exasperated, Mark's temper exploded. "To protect him from people like you! Now, get out!"

"All right. All right," the frustrated man responded as he backed out the door. He poked his head back inside. "But just wait till that town meetin'. You won't be sheriff after that—I guarantee it!"

Mark shut and locked the door after Toby left, then walked into the room with the cells. "I'm sure you must have heard, Troy."

"Yes, sir, I did."

"Don't let him bother you."

"Will he really make you lose your job—because of me?"

"Toby's an old windbag. You know that just from the short time you've been here. Nobody takes him seriously."

Troy sighed. "Do you think the judge will finish my trial?"

"I don't rightly know, Troy. He's going to be in town just until the end of the week. I'm sure he'll make a decision before then. He won't keep you locked up in here until the next time he comes through."

"I—I noticed ..." Troy ran his tongue nervously across his lips, "I noticed the gallows were still up."

Mark looked at him sympathetically. "Yeh. I guess it's just a waiting game. From the way I understand it, the Marshall boy is the one who brought the charges against you. So, he'd have to drop those charges for the judge to set you free. Otherwise, I'm thinking your trial will continue—soon."

Troy glumly shook his head, "Rod will never drop the charges. He hates me."

"Mmm. He seems to have a fair share of pride, too. But," Mark continued brightly, "miracles do happen. At least, isn't that what you and your family believe? Maybe it's time to put that faith of yours to the test—again."

Troy grinned sheepishly. "Yes, sir."

Mark turned to leave.

"Sheriff, just one more thing. Mama was here earlier, but I didn't want to ask her. I thought it might be too upsetting. How's Pop?"

"Still the same as far as I know," Mark replied. "You might add him to your prayers."

"I pray for him lots every day," Troy said, remembering his promise to Mom.

"I think restoring Pop to what he was will take another miracle. It's pathetic to see him like that. He's been such a bright spot in this town. He and Mom both. Everyone misses her terribly. But Pop—I think a part of him died with her."

"I think you're right."

"Well, goodnight, boy. And remember, don't let Toby get to you."

"I won't, Sheriff. Thank you."

CHAPTER 25

A New Charge

Not knowing what the judge would decide, Mark felt it was essential to allow Mary and Angie to visit Troy as frequently as they desired. He also managed to keep Toby at bay.

Troy spent most of the next couple of days, when he was alone, sharing his thoughts and fears with God and memorizing verses about trust.

After breakfast on the third day, the sheriff came to Troy's cell door toying with the handcuffs he'd gotten out of his desk drawer.

Troy gave him a quizzical look. "Where are you taking me? Is my trial back on?"

"The judge wants to see you for sentencing, son."

"Sentencing? But ... I never had a chance to defend myself!"

"I'm sorry, Troy. It's what I was told to do," Mark answered solemnly. "I can't cuff you with that sling on. Can I trust you not to run?"

"I won't run, Sheriff, but—"

"Let's go," Mark said abruptly, motioning for Troy to exit the cell.

Troy tried to wrap his mind around what was happening. *Am I not to be given a fair trial? Pa admitted he was the one who killed Jessica. Why am I being sentenced before I'm able to finish my defense?*

Poor Mama and Angie—to live through this another time! One favorable consideration pierced through his foreboding thoughts. *Maybe the judge is just going to declare me to be innocent. Maybe there has to be an official declaration before this nightmare is over.*

When they entered the church, the only people present were the judge, his mother and Angie, Rod and his mother, and Rachel and her father.

Why is Angie here? Surely Mama wouldn't make her listen to me being sentenced to death! He glanced around at the empty pews. *Why isn't anyone else here? Where are the jurors?*

"Did the sheriff tell you why I sent for you, young man?" Judge Taylor asked.

"Yes, sir," Troy replied quietly.

"I felt, under the circumstances, that a private sentencing would be in order. Is there anything you'd like to say before I pass judgment?"

There were plenty of questions Troy wanted to ask, but instead, he turned to Clara Marshall. "Mrs. Marshall, I—I didn't ... I want you to know that my pa and his men forced me to go that night. I know I had that sack of things from your house, but, as I said at my first trial, ma'am, after the ..." He paused, finding it difficult to bring up the traumatic event, "after the shooting happened, I was so scared I took the bag with me when I ran. I didn't even realize I had it until I got home. I knew it would make me look guilty, so I hid it, hoping I could somehow return the things to you later. I didn't even know Jessica was ..." He bit his lip, unable to say the word *dead.* "I should have stayed to see if I could help her. I was just so scared! My pa and his men must have gotten out of your house by the front door. What I mean is, I don't know what you saw or think you saw, but I didn't—"

"I know you didn't," Clara said tearfully.

"What? You *know*? But I thought—"

"I came here to testify against you because I saw how frustrated and angry Rod was over the death of his sister. I've never seen him in such a state of rage. It—it frightened me. I was so overcome with

150

grief." Tears were streaming down her face. "I had already lost my daughter. I was afraid I would lose my son, too. He was convinced you had done it. I thought, if—if you paid for the crime, it would give Rod peace. I know that's a terrible reason. It was a terrible thing for me to do! I was desperate! I wasn't thinking straight! My conscience has been relentlessly hounding me. I finally came to the judge yesterday and told him the truth. I'm so ashamed!"

"Rod's mother *was* an eyewitness," the judge explained. "Apparently, her daughter was not the only one who heard noises and got up to investigate. Mrs. Marshall was at the top of the stairs when the shot was fired. It was dark where she was standing, so you couldn't see her. However, she could clearly see you and your father because of the moonlight coming through the window. What she saw, however, was what you stated at your trial, that you tried to grab the gun away from your father—that you tried to protect her little girl."

"I even heard you begging your pa not to shoot. I'm so sorry, Troy!" Clara cried, "Can you ever forgive me?"

Troy sighed with relief; he'd been exonerated! "Yes. Yes, Mrs. Marshall. I can't imagine what you've been through—what my pa put you through. I'm just sorry I wasn't able to save Jessica."

"I came so close to destroying your life and the lives of my dear friend, Mary, and little Angie."

Mary gave Clara a comforting hug. "It's all right, Clara. Any of us might have done the same thing in your shoes."

"You wouldn't have. I know you wouldn't. You've always been such a dear. And to think how I've ignored you through the years and almost took your son's life! You have fine children, Mary. They're a tribute to you."

Rachel's father spoke next. "I don't know what to say, Troy. I was quick to condemn you, not because of who you are, but because of whose son you were. I hope you can find it in your heart to forgive me, as well."

"I knew you were just trying to protect Rachel," Troy responded as he shook the hand extended to him.

"I'm sorry I doubted you, son," Mr. Wagner added.

"Thank you, sir." A glimmer of hope that he and Rachel would spend the rest of their lives together flickered in his heart. He stifled it. Even though her father had made amends, it was a far cry from allowing his daughter to take on the last name of Daniels.

Rod's heart was pounding; his face flushed. The wrath that had burned within him was replaced with shame. "I have nothing to say that justifies what I've done, Troy." He studied a knot in the floorboard, unable to look at his former friend. "Everything you've suffered for the past few months is because of me. I'm the one who brought charges against you—both times. I came close to lynching ..." Rod broke down in tears. "At first, I did it for my mother, for Jessica. Then I became obsessed with making someone pay! Anyone! I convinced myself you were guilty even though I should have known better. I can't even beg for your forgiveness because I—I don't deserve it." He fell to his knees. "I'm so sorry, Troy! I'm so sorry! Not just for this but for the years of scorn, the ridicule ... I've been a prideful, snobbish idiot."

Of all the people who had opposed him, Rod had been the hardest for Troy to forgive. But seeing his former best friend in total brokenness brought tears to Troy's eyes and a lump in his throat. He reached down and helped Rod to his feet. "You're forgiven, Rod."

Everyone was tearful by this time, including Judge Taylor. "Since the plaintiff has dropped the charges brought against you, I proclaim you, 'Not guilty!'"

Troy had prepared himself for the worst; his relief made him feel weak. Yet, there was still one thing that bothered him. "Sir, I do have one concern."

"Go on," the judge encouraged Troy, clearing his throat to regain his composure. "You're free to speak your mind."

"Well, with just these few people here ... well, sir, I'd like everyone to know I'm innocent."

"They'll know soon enough!" Angie piped up. "All we need to do is tell one person!"

"Toby!" everyone said in unison.

The judge cleared his throat again. "Now, to get on with the sentencing."

"I know I broke into the Marshall home, but I already explained—"

"It's not that. Now, if you'll just let me get on with it."

Troy's face betrayed his total confusion. "But, sir, you just declared me to be innocent."

"You've had your chance to speak, son," the judge said sternly. "The defense will now be silent."

Troy looked at Mary, hoping she would step in and make sense of what was going on. Mary wasn't able to return the gaze. She looked away and stifled a chuckle.

"I find the defendant guilty as charged and sentence him to life." With that, he brought his gavel down against the pulpit.

Troy's thoughts were troubled, his heart beating uncontrollably. *Why doesn't someone stand up for me? Why hasn't Rachel said anything on my behalf?* "But, sir—" he muttered.

"Let me finish. The charge has changed."

Troy was thoroughly bewildered by this time as Angie giggled, and everyone else broke into broad smiles.

"The charge is that you are in love with one Rachel Wagner. Now, how do you plead to that?"

Troy shook his head in astonishment; his body relaxed. Rachel came close to him and slipped her hand into his. "Sentenced for life, sir?" He grinned at the judge's clever play on words.

Judge Taylor's eyes twinkled as a mischievous smile spread across his face.

"It's all right, son. I approve," Mr. Wagner interjected.

Glancing over at Rachel, Troy lightly squeezed her hand; his heart started thumping again, only this time, he welcomed it. "I plead guilty, sir," he admitted to the judge, "and gladly accept the sentence."

"I understand you had to postpone your wedding plans. Is that correct?"

"Yes, sir."

"Well," the judge continued, "I will only be in Spring River until the end of this week. In light of that fact, your fiancée asked me to include, as a part of your sentence, a wedding to be held right here this Saturday."

Troy looked at Rachel again. "Oh, really?" he said, arching one eyebrow.

"Besides," the judge continued, "after everything that's happened, I think Spring River could use a wedding!"

Everyone began talking at once as they exited the church.

The ladies began making plans.

"I want to purchase the material for your dress, Rachel," Clara offered. "It's the least I can do."

"The mercantile should have some white fabric that will work," Mary said. "And I saw a bit of white lace trim with the yard goods."

"There's no dressmaker's shop in town, is there?"

"No, Rachel," Mary responded.

"Maybe the tailor?"

"Definitely *not* the tailor!" Mary shuddered to think of Toby making Rachel's dress. She assumed they couldn't keep him from coming to the ceremony, but she would make sure he had no part in it.

"I'm good with a needle and thread," Clara remarked.

"I am, too," Mary added.

"I can sew a little," Rachel laughed.

Mary was delighted to be adding Rachel to her family. "Between the three of us, we'll make you the most gorgeous wedding dress ever!"

Rachel was skeptical. "In just two days?"

"In just two days," Clara and Mary answered in unison.

The judge accompanied Mark to the sheriff's office. They would need to wire other towns to inform them the case was closed and the wanted posters with Troy's picture should be destroyed.

Troy stayed behind for a few minutes to chat with his future father-in-law. "I can't tell you how grateful I am, sir," he said, extending his hand. "I love your daughter very much, and I promise I'll do everything in my power, with God's help, to give her a good life."

Mr. Wagner clasped Troy's hand warmly and gave it a firm shake. "I know you will, son. Again, please forgive me—"

"There's no need, sir. You're already forgiven. We can put the past behind us."

"I'd like nothing better. A fresh start would be best." He shook Troy's hand again, then headed to the hotel. The last few months had been long and emotional. It was time for a rest.

Troy thought about how quickly life could change, sometimes for the worse, sometimes for the better. It suddenly dawned on him that, in just two days, he would have to provide for a wife. He would talk with his mother about it. *Perhaps she and Angie can live in the spare room in Pop's apartment and be responsible for his care. That would leave the downstairs room for Rachel and me, and we could manage the store.* It seemed like the perfect solution.

"Troy," Rod's voice interrupted his musings.

"Rod. I thought you had gone."

"No, I've been out on the front steps thinking about how you've forgiven us." He ran his fingers back through his hair and sighed. "Could we talk?"

"Of course." Troy motioned toward the wooden bench in the front of the church.

Rod sat down next to Troy, putting his elbows on his knees and his head in his hands. "I—I'm not sure how to say this. I think it's going to come out all wrong, but I've got to do it." He looked at Troy. "I've thought about how I would have reacted if you had falsely accused me of ... murder. Or if *you* had tried to take *my* life for a crime I hadn't committed. And I—I couldn't have done what

155

you did. I couldn't have forgiven you. I would have wanted you to pay.

"I know you and your ma and sister have a lot of faith—"

"I'm afraid our faith wavered at times," Troy said.

"It might have wavered, but it was still there. I made fun of you for believing in God, for thinking He could or would help you. But now, I realize you have something I don't have. Something I need. Something that gave you the ability to forgive when you should be hating me."

Troy put his hand on Rod's shoulder. "A person has to humble himself to come to God. Maybe it took all this to bring you to that point. I would love nothing better than to tell you how you can have that same faith."

CHAPTER 26

The Wedding

Time seemed to crawl by on the stumpy feet of a tortoise yet fly by on the swift wings of an eagle until Saturday finally arrived.

The day seemed surreal to Troy. He was amazed at how fickle human nature could be. Not long before, most of the people attending the wedding had been at his trial. Then, they had wanted him to be hanged. Now, they were smiling, happily conversing, and wishing Rachel and him the best. However, he could tell by the scowl on Toby's face that at least one in the audience was not pleased. He decided to ignore the temptation to dwell on Toby's negativity. This was his and Rachel's special day; he would not let anything or anyone ruin it.

It was time for the ceremony. Troy stood beside Rod, his best man, and marveled at the difference in his friend. *Only by the grace of God*, he thought. Clara sat in the front beside Mary. She gave him an affirming nod. Mary turned to watch Angie as she came down the aisle bearing a bouquet of wildflowers. The judge took his place behind the pulpit and asked everyone to stand as Rachel, dressed in a simple but elegant gown edged with white lace, walked to the front with her father. Troy gazed at her, transfixed, thinking he had never seen any woman as beautiful.

After everyone was seated, Judge Taylor began, "We are gathered here today for the marriage of Troy Robert Daniels and Rachel Marie Wagner. If there is anyone present who knows why these two should not be joined in holy matrimony, speak now or forever hold your peace."

Immediately, Toby sprang to his feet. "I know a reason!"

A hush fell over the room, followed by murmuring.

"Have you people forgotten so quickly that this boy's trial was never finished? What will happen to this town if the likes of him takes up residence here?"

"The town will be a lot better off," Mark shouted to a response of nervous laughter among the attendees.

"Mark my words," Toby persisted, undaunted in his task. "This is a sad day for Spring River!" He stomped out the door, making sure his boots made as much clatter as possible on the wooden floor.

Troy's face was crimson.

The judge looked over the crowd. "Charges were dropped against this young man. We all know who admitted to the crime. End of story. We have a wedding to perform!"

Although the service continued without incident, Troy was on edge, barely hearing what was being said until the judge announced he could kiss his bride. All thoughts of Toby and the past vanished as he looked deeply into Rachel's bright blue eyes, then tenderly kissed her lips.

Rachel threw her arms around him, careful not to put pressure on his bad shoulder, and whispered into his ear. "Finally—a time for us!"

As the judge introduced them to everyone as "Mr. and Mrs. Troy Daniels," Troy silently assured himself that the God Who had made this impossible moment possible would also guide the future.

Interesting Sidenotes

*If you're looking for more—the answer is "Yes! I am planning to write a sequel!"

Have you ever wondered how an author chooses some names or dates? In this story, January 8th is significant. I chose it because it's the birthdate of my husband and my brother, and it fits the timeline. The name Marie was used for Rachel's middle name because my middle name is Marie, as was my mother's, my mother-in-law's, my daughter's, etc. You get the picture! The name Henry has also been popular with our family. However, since I'm not fond of the name (no offense to anyone reading this whose name is Henry), I chose Robert (my brother's first name—whose middle name is, you guessed it, Henry). Jed, one of Wilbur's hunting dogs, was named for my grandsons' HUGE—and I mean HUGE Saint Bernard/Great Dane.

If you enjoyed this story, it would be a personal blessing to me, and a help to others, if you would take a few minutes to leave a rating and/or review on the Amazon product page, Goodreads, Bookbub, etc. Also, if you can give a shout-out to your friends on social media, it will help spread the word! Thank you so much!

About the Author

Sandi Rebert is the wife of pastor Brian Rebert. Together, they have ministered in rural Maine for over forty years.

Sandi has written over twenty Christian plays, cantatas, programs, and musicals, which have been presented by churches across the United States and in several other countries. She is presently turning her most popular dramas into novels. In addition, teaching private music lessons led to the writing of a Christian piano course, Praising God on the Piano. Sandi has also been published in the past in several national Christian magazines.

She also enjoys art, playing various musical instruments, acting, and homeschooling, The Reberts have three grown children and six precious grandchildren.

To explore or purchase Sandi's plays or music, please visit her website: https://www.dramaticdifference.com. To purchase or read her other books, click on the Amazon product pages under the book descriptions on the following pages.

Also By Sandi Rebert

Born in a London workhouse, John has suffered years of physical and verbal abuse. Finally managing to escape, he stows away on a ship bound for the colonies, only to be discovered while out at sea. After another failed attempt at freedom, he is sold as an indentured servant to the bootmaker in Williamsburg, Virginia. His new-found faith in Christ is tested daily by his master's arrogant son. Then Elizabeth walks into his life . . . (A Christian Historical Romance Novel)

Reviews:

"I absolutely adored In Due Season!! The author did an amazing job writing the characters. I started to feel as though they were real people instead of just characters in a book. I had so many emotions reading this book. And there were so many unexpected twists, which I love in a book."

"Wow! A friend recommended this to me, and I am so glad she did. I laughed, I cried, my jaw dropped, and I was sad to see it end. There were several quotes I highlighted as inspiration. The author definitely did her research and made you feel as though you were living in colonial times, even giving nods to certain signers of the Declaration of Independence. Her descriptions create a great mind movie without filling in too many blanks. Upon finishing, I immediately checked to see if she has other novels published and I was thrilled to see that she does."

It's 1876 in Philadelphia, Pennsylvania. The Centennial Exhibition is the largest in the country! Against this backdrop of excitement, creativity, and technological innovations, two hurting souls meet at Hope Mission in the heart of the city's slum district. Both are seeking God's direction for the future. Both desperately need to forgive. (A Christian Historical Novella with a Touch of Romance.)

Reviews:

"Sandi has the talent to descriptively write of people and places so well that you feel you are actually in the story. With the addition of historical references and Biblical truth, it all adds up to a book you won't be able to put down."

"My attention was pulled in and kept there as I read. In these days of so much hurt and heartache, this is a much-needed story of forgiveness. Sandi is an excellent writer, skillfully drawing the picture and setting the scene with her words."

AN AWARD-WINNING NOVEL, Redemption's Promise is an exciting adventure/romance set in Jerusalem during Jesus' death through His ascension. It also weaves in Old Testament prophecies and their fulfillment in Christ. All this in a fast-paced fictional story you won't be able to put down!

Jason bar Micaiah is just sixteen years old. His father, an insurrectionist, has been killed; his mother is missing. Given the choice of death, slavery, or becoming the son of a Roman centurion—he chooses adoption. Though he despises his new identity, his secret goal is to use it to his advantage and continue his father's fight against Roman tyranny. Jason's life becomes an exciting, dangerous, and soul-searching adventure that ultimately leads to the true meaning of Redemption's Promise.

Reviews:

"The author has penned a spectacular and authentic historical story which includes kindness, love. forgiveness, struggles, and an ever-present thread of Jesus' life, love, and influence."

"Best historical fiction I have ever read!"